Our Land of Darkness

Welsh Myths, Legends and Ghost Stories

Nic Cunningham

Updated version
ISBN-13: 978-1-913297-22-0
Ebook:978-1-913297-23-7
Previously published by Nic Cunningham
ISBN-13: 979-8-592483-57-8

Saron Publishers
Pwllmeyrick House
Mamhilad
Mon
NP4 8RG

www.saronpublishers.co.uk
info@saronpublishers.co.uk
Follow us on Facebook and Twitter

Cover design by © Tassam Designs 2021

By the same author

Strange Tales From Wales
Dark Tales From Wales
Cymru Am Byth
A Poetic Walk Through Wales
The Last Train Home
Celestial Event
Giovanni and Domenico
The Short Book of Welsh Phrases

More from Saron Publishers

Fiction

Sent With Love	Children of Caerleon
King Henry VIII	David Collard
Summer Season	Darcy Drummond
Water of Life	Darcy Drummond
Frank	Julie Hamill
Jackie	Julie Hamill
The Ruminations of Bing	Tim Harnden Taylor
The Meanderings of Bing	Tim Harnden Taylor
The Ramblings of Bing	Tim Harnden Taylor
Penthusiasm	Penthusiasts of Usk

Non Fiction

The Fair Hollow	EJ Baldock
Exploring New Market Street	John Barrow
The Best of Times	Eugene Barter
Patron Saints of Gwent Churches	J Daryll Evans
Newport Operatic Society	David Kenny
A Trostrey Childhood	Graham Harris
Every Woman Remembered	Sylvia Mason
Real Murder Investigations	Kevin Moore
My Way	Kevin Moore
Good Cop, Bad Cop	Kevin Moore
Minstrel Magic	Eleanor Pritchard

OUR LAND OF DARKNESS

Welcome to *Our Land of Darkness*. Wales is a culturally rich nation, with a great future and an incredible past. The following stories and tales are intentionally eclectic. One tale you may be in modern day Cardiff, whilst the next in 19th century Wrexham.

Ghosts, Myths and Legends, Wales has all of them.

MEGAN'S MOBILE

CARDIFF

A few years ago, a friend's cousin bought a new mobile phone. After a long day of work in Cardiff, she came home, placed her phone on the counter and went watch to TV. When her son asked if he could play with her new phone, she agreed as long as he didn't call anyone or mess with text messages.

At around 11.20, she was drowsy, so she decided to tuck her son in and go to bed. She walked to his room and saw that he wasn't there. She ran over to her room to find him sleeping on her bed with the phone in his hand.

Relieved, she picked her phone back up from his hand to inspect it. Browsing through it, she noticed only minor changes such as a new background and banner, but then she opened her saved pictures. She began deleting the pictures he had taken, until only one new picture remained.

When she first saw it, she was in disbelief. It was her son sleeping on her bed, but the picture was taken by someone else above him . . . and it showed the left half of an elderly woman's face.

THE DARK CASTLE

CAREW

Carew is the setting for one of Pembrokeshire's best known ghost stories. In the 17th century, Carew Castle was home to bad-tempered drunk Sir Roland Rhys, who kept a pet ape named Satan. Satan had been captured from a shipwreck and Sir Roland kept it chained up in the castle's northwest tower for the entertainment of guests.

One day, his son eloped with the daughter of a local Flemish merchant who, furious about the loss and dishonour of his daughter, stormed the castle to accost Sir Roland. This merchant also rented land from Sir Roland and, because of the insult to his daughter, refused to pay the money due. Enraged equally by the attack on his son and the loss of his rent money, Roland freed the ape and, using a lighted taper, goaded him to attack the merchant.

The attack was so savage that the man almost died. But as he managed to make his escape, he cursed Sir Roland that he might suffer the same fate.

That night, staff in the castle heard terrible screams coming from the northwest tower where a fire was raging. When they rushed to the tower, they found Sir Roland lying dead in a pool of blood, his throat ripped open. It was obvious that the ape had turned on his master, thus fulfilling the prophecy. The ape was also found dead. On certain nights, it's claimed the ghost of the ape can be seen prowling the battlements and howling into the night.

It may be scary to see a ghost, but to see the ghost of an ape surely would be terrifying.

Another ghost haunts Carew. Princess Nest, who seems to have bestowed her favours far and wide, became the lover of Henry 1, by whom she bore a son, before being married off to Gerald of Windsor, bringing him Carew Castle as part of her dowry. Five children and nine years later, Owain ap Cadwgan, a Prince of Ceredigion, captured her. Before Henry 1's intervention freed her, she had borne Owain two children.

After Gerald's death, Nest married Stephan, Castellan of Cardigan, by whom she had several more children. After she died, her spirit remained chained to the earth and the shimmering form of the White Lady has been seen drifting along the passages and staircases of Carew. Her white figure was once seen to appear in a group photograph taken on a children's visit to the castle.

THE BRIDE OF DEATH

NANT GWRTHEYRN

The secluded village of Nant Gwrtheyrn is home to one of the most tragic ghost stories to have emerged from North Wales – and it all stems from an age-old tradition, the Wedding Quest.

Rhys and Meinir were childhood sweethearts, practically inseparable, with their favourite spot being under an old oak tree on the slopes of Yr Eifl. As they grew, their love became stronger and finally, the time came for them to be married.

The day before the wedding, which was to be at Clynnog Church, neighbours and guests brought gifts to present to the happy couple. That evening, while Rhys and Meinir were sitting under the old oak tree, Rhys carved their names into the tree trunk. This upset Meinir who believed it was bad luck to do this before they were married, but Rhys assured her that no bad luck would ever happen to them.

All seemed well – until the next morning.

A local tradition, the Wedding Quest, involved the bride hiding from her groom on the morning of their wedding. The guests waited in the church for Meinir to be found by Rhys and his friends, who would then take her to the church where they would be wed. Meinir had been seen heading for the hills so that's where Rhys and his friends started their search in high spirits. But no one could find her. As the day wore on, and Rhys became more and more panicked, he began to realise that Meinir was gone – maybe for good.

Over the next few months, Rhys continued his search. He grew gradually more desperate, eventually becoming a wild man of the woods, losing his mind completely.

One stormy night, months after Meinir had disappeared, Rhys took shelter under their favourite oak tree. A bolt of lightning struck the tree as he cowered beneath it, splitting the trunk wide open. Within the splintered oak were the remains of his bride-to-be, still wearing her wedding dress.

Rhys' shock and grief overcame him, and he died on the spot next to his Meinir.

There have been reports of their ghosts haunting the site ever since – a skeleton in a wedding dress, holding hands with a dishevelled wild man. It is also believed that no birds will land on the bark of the hollow tree, except the owl and the cormorant.

A memorial to the couple now stands on Yr Eifl.

WHERE THE CROW FLIES,

THE RAVEN DIES

PONTNEWYDD VILLAGE 1997

Well-known in the village of Pontnewydd, an old brick bridge spans the Great Western Railway tracks. November 6th, 1977 was a typical wet and soggy evening, still with the slight smell of fireworks and bonfires in the air from the parties the night before. Clouds covered the skies and there was no moon, and a howling wind was being pushed under the old railway bridge.

A few locals, after finishing off the evening with a few pints, had just left one of the local pubs and were walking down Station Road over the hill. Then a scream chilled their bones.

The scream sounded like that of a young woman. It appeared to be coming from the railway tracks beneath the bridge. They looked down towards the tracks and saw a young woman in her late 20s running across the railway line.

One of the men shouted, 'Are you OK, love?' There was no reply.

Wanting to help a lady in distress, the three men jumped over the fence and made their way through nettles down the embankment towards the railway lines.

Once near the tracks, they searched for the woman, and soon spotted her again running on the tracks. They all called after her. At that point, the men later described the feeling of a cold ache running through their bodies and became keenly aware of someone behind them. Slowly turning, each of the men looked back towards the village and the railway bridge.

About 25 metres away, between them and the bridge, they saw the woman again. From head to toe she was drenched in blood.

Shocked by what they saw, the men retreated in fear, before one of the men asked, 'What happened to you?'

The woman replied, 'Where the crow flies, the raven dies.' She then repeated this. 'Where the crow flies, the raven dies.'

The men were now frozen in fear, realising that the woman in front of them was no longer in distress and they were in fact experiencing something from the dark world.

'Who are you?' asked one of them, to which she replied, 'I was Lady Charlotte, now I am the daughter of death.'

The men could not take any more and fled in terror. The next day, they told the story to friends and family, most of whom believed they had indeed had one too many a pint and did not believe them, thinking the stories were a prank conjured up by the three friends.

1988

As they were returning from Friday night fun at Ashley House Youth Centre, two young lads, walking down the hill into Pontnewydd village, claimed they'd seen a woman in a white dressing gown, covered in blood. Scared, the teenagers ran off, and told their parents what they had seen.

1997

At about 1.30am, a taxi driver was finishing up on a night spent ferrying folks around Cwmbrân. It was a cold November night. Driving into Pontnewydd, he noticed a man walking on the pavement in what looked like Edwardian clothing. The taxi driver chuckled to himself as he carried on driving. About a mile further on, up the very steep Trappas Hill, the driver saw a lady apparently in distress, with a long white robe and red paint or blood on her.

Shocked, he pulled over to look back at the lady he had driven past to see if she needed assistance. When he looked back, he was stunned to see that she had gone, but, with an icy chill down his spine, he was looking directly at the man in Edwardian clothes he had passed a few moments before.

The man began walking directly towards the taxi. In horror, the taxi driver fled the scene.

There have been several other sightings of the lady since these events, but none of the man in Edwardian clothing.

THE WOODS

WEST OF PONTYPOOL

There have been several sightings over the years of a lady in the woods west of Pontypool. She seems to be wearing a tall hat and a black dress and moves in a strange motion, almost like a drunken stagger. On all occasions, the lady is followed by a large black dog. Sightings of this woman and a dog go back as far as the 1600s and were still happening even up to the 1990s.

In the spring of 1998, a jogger, who lived nearby, was running through the woods west of the town, near an area known locally as the Tranch.

It was midday and a sunny blue-sky day. As the runner started making his way up a small rise, suddenly in front of him appeared a very tall gaunt-looking lady. As in previous sightings, she was wearing a long black dress and a strange tall hat that resembled a crown.

He noticed that her colour and complexion were very pale, gaunt, even malnourished. He froze in his tracks as the lady looked directly at him, saying later that 'It was like she was looking right through me.'

He stood about 50 yards away from the lady, and then noticed a very large jet-black dog behind her. He believed the dog was a rottweiler, but very much larger. Even from where he was standing, he could see large spike-like teeth protruding from the dog's mouth.

An icy chill coursed down through his spine. As he started to return the way he'd come, the lady stretched out her arm towards him and pointing with a finger, said, 'Tywyllwch.'

The word commonly means *darkness* in Welsh. The man began to run but his legs were weak, as fear gripped him. He managed to run 200, maybe 300, metres before he stopped and looked back but no trace of the lady or the dog could be seen.

The day now turned dreary, wet and very misty. Cold hung in the air, while dew clung to the leaves and grass all around him. In the far distance, he could hear a dog barking.

Since that day, there have been fourteen other sightings of the lady and her dog - that's right, fourteen. This is a major paranormal event.

Little is known of the lady and her dog. One story we do have is that in the 15th century, a local nobleman married a rich young lady of France. They were married in France without the knowledge of her family. They then travelled back to Wales where they began living in the Pontypool area. The story goes that her family in France, ashamed by her marriage to a non-French gentleman, hired an assassin to have the lady killed. The chosen person was a Welsh woman by the name of Grilliog who was known for carrying out such tasks.

One late autumn afternoon, Grilliog had traced the whereabouts of the young couple, and approached the village of Pontypool near the West Woods. Nearing the couple's home, a large beast of unknown identity attacked and killed her.

Unfortunately, we know very little else other than the beast was also killed in the attack by Grilliog's knife. Could this beast be the dog that is seen in the woods, that somehow in death, both beast and Grilliog now must spend eternity with each other?

If you see this woman and dog near Pontypool, beware. Several eyewitnesses have been in terrible accidents within days of seeing her.

LLANCAIACH FAWR MANOR

TRELEWIS

1960 1988 1989 2001

Llancaiach Fawr is one of the most haunted houses in Wales. Strange goings on have been reported in nearly every room of the house which is now open to the public as a living museum.

Mattie was the housekeeper at Llancaiach Fawr Manor for many years. After her death, which came about after she was burned in an accident, the manor was said never to be the same again. Her bedroom in particular affects visitors with a crushing sense of sadness, even reducing tough Australian rugby players and senior police officers to tears. She appears down the manor's dark hallways on Thursday nights, and on those nights alone. She has been seen washing windows, brushing floors and even serving tea. Little is known about this ghost, although she is obviously a faithful servant as she continues serving after her death.

Another ghost is that of a young boy who died when he fell from the first floor onto the flagstones below in 1906. He tends to make his presence known by tugging at visitors' dresses or trying to hold their hands. Several other ghostly children delight in playing pranks on the staff, and costumed guides have long grown used to their aprons being untied by teasing ghostly children. One staff member, walking down a staircase, was terrified to find a cold childish hand under his when he placed his hand on the banister.

Yet another ghost is the figure of a hooded girl on the cellar steps which was seen by one of the guides at the house. A few years later, one of the visitors on a ghost tour claimed that a young girl was following this guide around the house. When asked to describe the girl, she gave a description which matched exactly with the hooded girl the guide had seen a few years earlier.

Disembodied voices are regularly heard in the 'next room', even surfacing on the soundtrack of a television programme made at the house. Disappointed at the short segment which appeared when the programme was broadcast, staff at the house were dumbfounded to learn that much of the tape had to be discarded as there 'were foreign voices drowning out the presenters. The 'foreign' language in question was presumably Welsh.

MARGAM COUNTRY PARK

NEATH PORT TALBOT

Margam Castle is an impressive and dramatic site with unique architectural features. Over the years, many strange occurrences have been reported from this imposing building, making it a strong contender for the UK's most haunted house.

Often the ghostly activity has been described as violent and terrifying. People visiting the heart of the old building have reported seeing orbs, feeling cold chills, hearing unexplained noises and seeing objects move, as well as catching glimpses of ghostly figures in Victorian dress.

Probably the strangest of these tales and hauntings are those of children who have been seen in Victorian dress in various parts of the estate and house. There have even been reports of visiting children wandering off from their families and finding new friends to play with. What is particularly strange is that there is absolutely no evidence of any children ever dying at this location. So, the question remains, who were these children?

Another ghost who makes his presence felt frequently is that of gamekeeper Robert Scott who was murdered by a poacher and is so consumed by rage at his unjust killing that he still frequents the castle to this day, slamming doors and hurling rocks at anyone trying to get in contact with him.

Staff at the castle regularly see the figure of a blacksmith, while security guards have reported hearing running footsteps and chattering voices.

KINGS ARMS HOTEL

ABERGAVENNY 1971 2020

A popular place to eat, and to taste local ales, the King's Arms Hotel in Y Fenni is a late 16th century coaching inn and a great place to visit.

There have been sightings of a scullery maid and of an elegant woman totally dressed in black, descending the staircase and walking through the lounge. It is rumoured that she was raped by a monk who had been offered sanctuary at the inn. She became pregnant but died in childbirth and is thought to roam the inn, searching for the child she never got to hold.

ST CATHERINE'S ISLAND

PEMBROKESHIRE

Given the dangerous shores surrounding Wales, it's inevitable that many of its legends relate to the sea.

Visitors to Tenby very quickly notice St Catherine's Island, the crag of rock at the eastern end of South Beach, its dramatic outline topped by a massive Victorian fort. Very few people know the ancient legend of the lonely soul who once lived there, long before the fort was built.

The story begins in a violent storm that blew up without warning, one summer in the mid 1500s. The Tenby fishing vessels had left port as usual that morning, but as the storm threatened and the waves began to rise, their crews hauled in their nets and headed back to the shelter of the harbour.

Their families had gathered on Castle Hill, watching for their safe return. As the boats arrived safely one by one, the watchers noticed that, far out across the bay, another larger ship was struggling to reach shelter. Nobody recognised it as a local vessel, but it was noticeable that strange lights played across its decks and ghostly shapes seemed to be clinging to the rigging and the masts.

Although there was no one to be seen at the helm of the strange ship, something or someone seemed to be guiding it into the sands near St Catherine's Island.

As night fell, the vessel grounded with a sound like thunder, and though the watchers on Castle Hill rushed down to the beach to offer what help they could to the shipwrecked mariners, they could find no trace of the ship or its crew. Terrified, the people of Tenby fled back to their homes, but all through the night, strange sounds were heard coming from the shore and disembodied voices wailed in the wind.

By morning, the storm had died down and the day was bright and clear. In groups of two or three, people returned to the sands to see if there were any signs of the ghostly ship. Again, there was no trace of the wreck but they were astonished to find a man wearing strange clothes, lying in a deep sleep near the top of the beach.

He was taken into the nearest house where he was cared for, but when he awoke, he would tell them little of his background. He refused all offers of hospitality and retreated to St Catherine's Island, where he made his home.

The only person to whom he would speak was a local shepherd, who each day took him food and who, one day, learned something of his life. The man had led a murderous band of pirates who attacked and robbed ships along the coasts of Wales. Sadly, he recounted how, in a jealous rage, he had slain the person who had loved him most, after which, as a punishment, his ship was taken over by the spirits of those innocent sailors he had killed during his time as a pirate. It was these ghostly forms who had been visible as his ship approached the beach and who had caused the wreck.

The stranger explained that he was tormented by sea maidens, who rose from the waves with messages from his dead lover, assuring him that she was now happy and wanted him to join her. As he related this story, he suddenly sprang to his feet, shouting, 'I come, I come. Let me be with her, let me be at rest.' Before the startled shepherd could do anything, the stranger leapt from the cliffs of St Catherine's Island and was drowned.

THE ANGEL/MERMAID

ST DOGMAEL'S

One day during the 18th century, a young fisherman named Peregrine was casting his nets into the waters off Cemaes Head, in north Pembrokeshire. Not an educated man, Peregrine was nevertheless a good fisherman, like his father and grandfather before him, and understood the ways and moods of the sea.

Suddenly his nets tightened and he knew he had a good catch. Gradually he managed to haul the nets aboard the boat where, to his astonishment, he found not herring but a mermaid. He knew this catch was a real money spinner and quickly set sail back to St Dogmael's.

But his triumph was short-lived. The mermaid wept bitterly at being captured and begged him to let her go, saying her scales were cracking away from the water and that she would soon die. Entranced by her beauty, he was reluctant to agree but he realised it was the right thing to do. He cut her free from the nets and helped her back into the water, watching sadly as she disappeared beneath the waves.

Peregrine turned for home once more, only to find the mermaid had once again surfaced alongside his boat.

'You are a good man, Peregrine,' she said, and promised, as thanks, to give him three warning shouts when he was in the greatest danger of losing his life.

Many weeks passed by and there was no sign of the mermaid. Then, one still September day in 1789, he was again fishing off Cemaes Head when the mermaid suddenly appeared beside his boat.

'Peregrine! Peregrine! Peregrine!' she called. 'Take up your nets and go. Take up your nets. Take up your nets!'

Peregrine immediately did as he was bid and headed back to shore, despite the laughter of the other fishers. Shortly afterwards, the sky darkened and a violent storm arose. Many fishermen were drowned - 18 in some versions of the legend but church records place the number at 27 - but Peregrine was saved by the mermaid's warning.

HWCH DDU GWTA

PEMBROKESHIRE

For centuries, the people of Pembrokeshire have feared bumping into this huge black beast with red eyes, that seized souls to carry off to the underworld.

Hwch Ddu Gwta translates as the *Tailless Black Sow* and it's said that there's no escaping its clutches. It was thought to have haunted the banks of a stream near Narberth, terrifying local people to such an extent that, after dark, no one would cross the bridge that spanned the stream.

One brave local, full of alcohol after an evening session at the tavern, decided to ride his horse full pelt across the bridge in defiance of the story. Just to be certain of not seeing the beast, he kept his eyes closed and his head down as he galloped towards the crossing.

Unfortunately, the horse must have also closed his eyes because he missed the bridge completely and fell into the river, throwing the local into the icy waters.

When he surfaced, spluttering and gasping, there was the beast on the opposite bank, glaring straight at him. Terrified, he fled on foot back to the safety of the tavern, his screams waking people in every house he passed. It took him many months to recover from the shock and he never again ventured out at night. There is no record of what happened to the horse!

A similar tale about Y Hwch Ddu Gwta is told in North Wales where, on Nos Calan Gaeaf – October 31st – women and children danced around a village fire. Each person wrote their name on a rock and placed it in the fire. When the fire died down, the villagers raced home so that they wouldn't be caught by Y Hwch Ddu Gwta who would eat their souls. The following morning, the rocks were checked. A missing stone was thought to be a death omen.

THE LIGHTS

BROAD HAVEN

One of the most famous UFO sightings in the UK took place just over 40 years ago in the quaint little village of Broad Haven, on the west coast of Pembrokeshire.

In 1977, a class of pupils from Broad Haven Primary School said they spotted a UFO in a field near their playground. It sparked a wave of sightings for the rest of the year, leading the area to be dubbed the Dyfed Triangle.

The pupils described seeing a silver 'cigar-shaped' craft with a 'dome covering the middle third' and said they had 'a strange desire to run away'. They also described a silver-suited spaceman coming out of the spaceship. Naturally enough, their teacher didn't believe them and the school day continued as normal.

As the children left the school at the end of the day, they saw the spaceship again and told everyone what they had witnessed. Again, they were disbelieved so, the following day, upset at not being taken seriously, they demanded that the police investigate the incident properly.

Intrigued, the headmaster decided to do some investigating of his own. The children were separated and asked to draw what they saw. Oddly, they all drew the same shapes.

It started a year of many abnormal events. A local farming family saw UFOs, with a 7-foot-tall silver-suited spaceman with a black visor appearing outside the windows. Their car and television sets constantly broke down and had to be replaced and their cows mysteriously turned up in different fields.

Two months later, a hotel owner in nearby Little Haven described seeing an object which looked like an 'upside-down saucer' and two 'faceless humanoid' creatures with pointed heads in silver suits. She said so much heat came off it, her 'face felt burned. There was light coming from it and flames of all colours, then the creatures came out of these flames.' She called some hotel residents to see what she was witnessing but by the time everyone gathered at the window, there was no sign of the craft. When she later visited the field, she said there were 'two inches of burned ground'.

DINEFWR

CARMARTHENSHIRE 1980

Set in the middle of the 18th century landscape park of Dinefwr is Newton House which, it is rumoured, is haunted at night by Lady Elinor Cavendish.

Lady Elinor was betrothed to a man she didn't love and, to escape him, she sought refuge with her family at Dinefwr. However, she was followed by her enraged suitor, who caught up with her and strangled her to death, supposedly with her own hair ribbon. Overcome with guilt, her would-be suitor then killed himself.

Ever since then, muffled voices have reverberated around the empty rooms, and staff have reported lights being turned on and off. There are also numerous mysterious cold spots and from time to time, the unmistakeable aroma of pipe of cigar smoke where no one is smoking. This is thought to be the ghost of Walter, who worked at the house as butler. Rumours abound of a hanging in the house centuries ago, which again suggests the strangling feeling experienced by many visitors. A haggard old lady has often been seen at the top of the stairs and looks so ferocious that many visitors refuse to walk past her.

In the 1980s, a camera crew attempted to capture Elinor's ghost on film. Although they were unsuccessful, the members of the crew all fell ill, one after the other, one cameraman claiming that, while he was asleep in the very room where Elinor was reputedly murdered, he felt invisible hands squeezing his throat.

TŶ'R SGÊR

PORTHCAWL

Sker House dates back almost a thousand years to when it was first built by monks of the Cistercian order as a monastic grange to support nearby Margam Abbey. After the dissolution of the monasteries, ownership of the estate changed hands several times in quick succession whilst it remained a refuge for renegade monks.

In 1597, the then-owner, Jenkin Turberville, a staunch Roman Catholic, was allegedly tortured to death after being accused of promoting the 'Old Religion'. In 1679, the missionary St Philip Evans was hung, drawn and quartered in Cardiff after being arrested at Sker House the previous year. Many other dignitaries and prominent historical figures have spent time there, and visitors once travelled from far and wide to marvel at its spectral beauty.

As usual, the house is linked to a tragic love story. Elizabeth Williams, a daughter of the house, was in love with a local carpenter and harpist named Thomas Evans and they lost no time in becoming lovers. Despite her father Isaac disapproving, Elizabeth and Thomas planned to elope. Sadly for the lovers, as Thomas stealthily approached the house in a carriage and pair, the dogs alerted Isaac to the plot and he locked Elizabeth in her bedroom. To make matters even worse for Elizabeth, Isaac then married her off to Thomas Kirkhouse of Neath in a loveless union which she endured for nine years before dying of a broken heart in 1776. Her spirit is said to be unable to break free from Sker House and could account for visitors often experiencing a crushing sense of doom when entering the premises. If people move further into the house, high-pitched screams and wailing cries can be heard and witnesses speak of seeing a dark shadow in the corner of Elizabeth's bedroom.

Over the years, Sker House has become a hive of paranormal activity. People have reported seeing ghost ships just off the coast and disembodied lights flickering along the beach, as well as hearing mysterious banshee-like wailing sounds in the grounds. and there are also accounts of poltergeist activity and shadow people.

In Welsh mythology, many of these phenomena are considered portents of doom. The banshee-like wails could be attributed to an entity known as the cyhyraeth, traditionally prevalent along the Glamorganshire coast, which is said to be heard just before a shipwreck. Those even less fortunate would come face to face with the cyhyraeth. The creature could be either male or female, and is described as having wild, dishevelled hair, black pointed teeth, and long, withered arms. Death was said to follow in its wake, though rarely for the witness himself. Usually, a close friend or acquaintance would be claimed instead.

Likewise, the disembodied lights often seen around Sker could be examples of the dreaded canwyll corph (corpse candle or corpse light) in action. Appearing as single lights or in clusters, their size and brightness reflect the age of the victim, for whom these lights were said to signal imminent death. If the doomed person were female, the light would have a bluish hue. If male, it would be red. Sometimes, grinning skulls or even the features of the victim could be seen.

Again, the phenomenon is especially popular in coastal areas, and often said to be experienced in conjunction with the awful wails of the cyhyraeth. When seen on open ground, the canwyll corph are said to follow the exact route of the victim's funeral procession, which intriguingly ties in neatly with yet another popular legend of Sker.

One night early in the 19th century, a local man was returning home from work. His path took him along the beach. Glancing out at Sker Point, where the submerged ranks of sharp rocks jutted up from the seabed, he saw the shimmering wreck of a huge ship.

As he watched, a small group of translucent figures waded out to the vessel and carried something ashore. The shocked man couldn't see what the object was but guessed from its size and shape that it was a coffin. Fascinated, he followed the ghostly procession into town where, to his horror, it stopped outside his own house and vanished. A week later, a vessel was indeed wrecked off the coast of Sker and among the dead was the man's brother. When his body was recovered and taken back to the family home, the funeral procession took exactly the same route as the ghostly one he had witnessed.

Another supernatural phenomenon reported at Sker House is shadow people, a different, yet no less fascinating, proposition. Often glimpsed in one's peripheral vision, these entities, which resemble dark humanoid masses, are usually dismissed as mere products of the imagination or tricks of the light.

Shadow people are often linked to sleep paralysis and, in turn, alien abduction, with some of the more outlandish theories suggesting they could be time travellers from our own future. Even more disturbing is the fact that witnesses claim the interactions are becoming ever more terrifying, with the mysterious entities becoming more aggressive and confrontational. Whereas once they lurked in the shadows and were only glimpsed peeking out from around corners or disappearing through walls as if to evade detection, they now appear to be actively seeking people out. This indicates intelligence at work, rather than some kind of residual manifestation.

They are generally taken to be male, though lack any real gender-defining characteristics, and many witnesses report them as having red eyes, or somewhat bizarrely, wearing hats. Others are said to be hooded or cloaked, which has led some to suggest that there could be several distinctly different groups.

It is a misconception that all shadow people are evil. Some are considered fundamentally good and are looked upon as cosmic guardians. This would fit in with yet another school of thought which suggests they are elemental beings. Certainly, it's possible they have always been with us. Only in recent years have they really come to prominence, and numerous re-examinations of historical hauntings contain references to what we now call shadow people.

However, an alarming modern trend has seen not only the volume of sightings increase exponentially, but also the length and intensity of sightings. In the technological age, the sheer weight of evidence being amassed to support what sceptics originally dismissed as wild claims is overwhelming.

MAID OF CEFN YDFA

MAESTEG

In a tale very similar to that of The Maid of Sker, the Maid of Cefn Ydfa is probably more widely known and is based on a high degree of fact.

The legend says that Ann Thomas was placed in the wardship of Anthony Maddocks after her father's death. Anthony decided Ann was to marry his son, also Anthony. However, Ann was in love with the poet and thatcher Wil Hopcyn. Consequently, Anthony Snr locked her in her bedroom from where she wrote letters to Wil which a maid smuggled out and hid in the hollow of an oak tree. When her mother discovered this, she took away Ann's writing materials which led Ann to resort to writing messages in her own blood on leaves picked from a tree outside her window.

Unable to stand the separation, Wil left the area and Ann subsequently married Anthony Jnr. Legend has it that she pined so desperately for Wil that she fell seriously ill. On her death bed, she asked to see Wil and when he arrived, she died in his arms.

CASTELL-Y-ROCH

PEMBROKESHIRE

Roch Castle is said to be home to a number of spirits and otherworldly beings, and countless orbs and other minor paranormal activity have been reported, although the rumoured reason for the building of the castle may be stranger than anything which has happened there in the past eleven centuries.

According to legend, Adam de Rupe, the original owner of the castle, ordered it to be built after a witch prophesied that he would die from a snake bite within a year. However, the witch also promised Rupe that he would go on to live a long and healthy life if he managed to make it through the year without being bitten.

Determined to minimise his contact with venomous snakes, Rupe built Roch Castle and retired to its highest room, intending to stay there for the next 365 days.

Weeks turned into months and the seasons passed with little activity. Though Rupe's existence was boring, he found solace in the fact that he was still living and spent his time planning his return to the outside world.

Towards the end of the year, the winter weather made the castle almost too cold to inhabit, and so he sent a servant out for some wood so he could build a fire to warm himself. Unfortunately for Rupe, the wood had not been properly inspected and he wound up being bitten by a snake which had been lurking within the logs.

He died shortly afterwards and it is believed his ghost still haunts the castle, with the greatest amount of activity being reported on the higher floors of the building.

Among other reported ghosts is the spirit of Lucy Walter who was born in the castle in 1630. She became the mistress of Charles II, bearing him a son, James, Duke of

Monmouth. She has been seen, dressed in white, floating down the halls before disappearing without a trace. Guests at what is now a hotel claim to have heard disembodied footsteps during the night.

One of the men turned to another and in a voice that seemed dry and forced, said, 'He has seen the digger of Fotty.'

They began to converse in Welsh, the artist struggling in vain to understand what they were saying. But the men soon departed after many pitying glances and shaking of heads.

Sitting down to rest alongside the cottage owner, she began to explain.

The figure of the old man was that of someone who had perished several years ago. During his lifetime, he had been widely disliked and was said to, on more than one occasion, have taken the most relentless advantage of those experiencing financial difficulties.

His greed, his miserly behaviour and love of material possessions became an obsession which eventually culminated in a hallucination where he believed there was a vast treasure at Fotty – the place on the lake he was spotted.

At all hours, the old miser was seen digging in different places, despite the wind and adverse weather, delusional and muttering to an imaginary friend, which locals believed to be a fiend. This led to him being avoided and detested more than ever.

Eventually, on a stormy day, a fisherman discovered the old man's dead body at Fotty, with his spade still firmly in his grasp. Running to the nearest house to raise the alarm, a party of men returned to the spot, but by now, the body had vanished without a trace – spade and all – never to be seen again.

Some time later, the handle of the old man's spade was found in a virtually inaccessible hollow of the neighbouring mountains. The locals believed that the fiend with whom the old man had become so friendly had carried the miser's body over the mountains, dropping the spade along the way.

After this discovery, a farmer returning home late one night was almost frightened to death by witnessing what he took to be the ghost of the old miser, complete with spade in hand, digging for the elusive treasure.

The spectre of the old man was seen several times following this, with his appearance seen as warning of the direst calamity to those who saw him.

Certainly William Shrubsole died a mere three years later at the comparatively young age of 43.

REVENGE

CAERNARFON

A woman from Caernarfon, aged almost 100 years, recalled a story of revenge from beyond the grave.

In 1810, John Jones and his wife Jenny lived in a substantial farmhouse near Caeathro. Comparatively wealthy, the couple had an only daughter, named after her mother, Jimney. At the time the story opens, Mrs Jones had just died and her body lay in a room in the farm, awaiting burial. Her grave can be seen at Llanbeblig.

Near the Jones' farm stood the large house of Rhys Rhys, whose eldest son had fallen in love with the young Jimney Jones and had obtained Mr Jones' permission to marry her.

However, Mrs Jones had disliked the idea of a match between her pretty daughter and the sour heir of the neighbouring estate. Even up to her death, she had refused to withdraw her opposition and in this frame of mind had died, pronouncing a curse on the union if it were consummated after her death.

Ignoring her mother's wishes, Jimney proceeded to court young Rhys, enjoying frequent walks with him around the lanes. They vowed that they would marry. as soon as propriety would allow after her mother's funeral.

The day of the funeral arrived, wet and gloomy with fog. What was regarded as supernatural darkness surrounded the procession to Llanbeblig. The horrified mourners were also shocked at intervals by the apparent apparition of the late Mrs Jones, which appeared frequently during the march to the church, her spectre gleaming among the trees on the roadside.

The form of the woman claimed to promise doom on those who had so secretly determined to ignore her dying wishes. But the apparition disappeared quietly, and all returned home, soaked to the bone by the cold sleet that had fallen all morning, changing to heavy snow which covered the whole countryside.

Later only three people remained in Mr Jones' homestead. As the night drew in, Mr Jones offered Rhys a room, rather than let him face the terrors of the night on his journey home. Rhys gratefully agreed to stay the night. In a small room where a great wood fire burned, Jimney and Rhys sat together, talking about the day and the ghostly appearances of Mrs Jones during the funeral procession.

As the conversation continued, they became aware of a presence in the room and held their breath in fear.

There was nothing to be seen or heard, yet they felt that somewhere near them, an antagonistic supernatural presence was around them. The roaring fire suddenly waned and died. The watchers sat still in terror, staring into the gloom and clutching each other's hands. Every moment they expected some horrible vision to manifest in front of them, but there was no vision nor sound.

The long hours of the night passed and the three watchers, hand in hand, saw the day break with a shuddering cry of relief.

Three months later, Jimney and Rhys married and a large party gathered in the Rhys mansion, and song and dance rang through the old house.

At around eleven, the party ended, with old John Jones being the last to leave.

The newlyweds accompanied him to his now lonely house, waving goodnight on the doorstep. They slowly returned home, full of joy and hope for the future.

Upon their arrival, Jimney turned round to take one last look at her old home and immediately fell to the ground screaming. Rhys, who had turned to open the door, swung around to see what had terrified his new wife.

To his unspeakable horror, on the sill of his father in law's bedroom, burned the dim flame of the corpse candle. The deathly fear felt at the funeral began to fill the night air.

Outlined by the shadows stood the ghost of Jimney's mother, menacing but silent. Rhys stood paralysed with fear. The eyes of the apparition stared at him but with neither sound nor voice.

The moment was broken as he stooped to pick up his fallen wife. But the moment she turned her eyes to the hall door, a terrible cry rang through the night and she fell lifeless to the ground.

Lights now appeared and servants rushed to the front of the house. Rhys threw up his arms and fell beside his dead wife. When the servants carried the bodies into the house, life had passed from young Jimney. Fortunately, Rhys still lived, but his hair had turned completely grey.

THE NIGHT TERRORS

BERLLAN

Berllan, reached from Caernarfon by ferry, had remained empty for some time, the last residents long gone, and no one gave the house much of a passing thought.

Until one night, when a traveller who had passed the property ran into the town, drenched in his own urine.

Claiming every single window at the house was illuminated with a ghostly radiance, the man incontinently fled in terror, without making any attempt to discover the source of the lights. However, upon reaching town, he went on to tell several of his friends, who then formed a strict vigil - albeit at a distance - at the property for the succeeding nights.

However, the party of watchers saw nothing and belief in the man's story began to wane until another witness came forward, claiming to have seen the strange lights on another night and at a different time.

The vigils continued, with the result that it became clear that Berllan was nightly lit up with the mysterious fires.

On New Year's morning, a group of four people returning from the town saw the lights coming from the house. With safety in numbers, they made their way to the property to investigate but as they reached the house, the lights disappeared. As they retreated to the road, the house suddenly became ablaze with the same lights they had witnessed. As they ran back to Berllan, the lights disappeared once more, and the group found every door locked and the windows tightly shut.

After news of the ghostly lights spread, amateur investigator John Humphreys from Caernarfon decided to investigate. Knowing that the ghosts manifested themselves between seven in the evening and three in the morning, he was warned that the only evidence of their existence was the mysterious lights.

Upon arrival in the afternoon, he noted the house was set in the middle of an orchard, which at one point had been well kept. The one-storey building had all the blinds closed so it was impossible to peer in, and both windows and doors were firmly bolted. In the distance was a stable and a pigsty. Although the windows should have been easy to open, as they slid from side to side, rather than the more normal up and down, a long iron spoon had been placed in the groove and locked the windows in such a position that it was impossible to push them open.

Now knowing the layout of the land, John returned to town, with plans to go back to Berllan at midnight. Upon arriving back at Caernarfon, he bumped into a friend who agreed to accompany him. With apprehension that the ghosts would not appear if it were known when they were going, they kept their plans for the visit to the haunted house a secret.

At exactly midnight, he found his friend waiting patiently in the ferry with a particularly active and ferocious-looking bulldog by his side. Pushing away from the shore, the pair travelled silently across the water. It didn't take long to arrive at their destination.

The night was clear and a bright moonlight shone over the scene, dimmed at times by the flying clouds as they passed swiftly across the sky. A stiff breeze whistled through the hedges with a ghostly sound – appropriate, given the reason for their visit.

His companion lit a cigar, which glowed in the night as he puffed clouds of smoke and the unmistakable aroma into the night air while his brute of a dog trotted by his side in silence.

Upon arrival at the house, they could see it was in complete darkness. Intending to warn off any ordinary being who might be behind the mysterious lights, John loudly declared that he was carrying a revolver loaded with seven chambers and was also accompanied by a vicious bulldog.

Producing a skeleton key, they entered the building. Confronted by total darkness, John hesitated. However, his companion stepped boldly through the door. Striking a match, he lit a lantern and flashed the light over the interior.

The house was furnished plainly but comfortably. The kitchen table was laid out as if it was ready to serve supper but everything was covered in dust.

Passing into a bedroom, they noticed an ordinary oil lamp on the bedside table. Glancing at the window, they noticed the blind was drawn and that a thick set of curtains were on each side of the window.

Closing the curtains, they lit the oil lamp on the table.

Retreating into a corner, the dog began to growl, baring his teeth, his eyes darting out of his head. Back and back he cowered, terror depicted on his face. The wall stopped him retreating further, but he still cowered, cringing before the invisible terror which seemed to be advancing onto him. Shrinking to the ground, his growl transformed into a gasping, choking sound and his eyes strained fearfully upward.

The bedroom door opened and closed silently as a cold chill filled the room. Something had entered but they saw nothing, heard nothing. The men grasped at each other's outstretched hands in an attempt to dissipate the terror.

'What is it?' Humphreys asked.

'Get your revolver,' his friend replied.

The dog was still writhing in the corner, twisting his head around as if there was something trying to get behind him.

'Give me the revolver,' cried the friend sharply. 'Quick!'

At that moment, the lamp was suddenly extinguished and the men and the dog were plunged into darkness. But only for a moment.

The heavy curtains they had earlier drawn were thrust aside instantaneously but silently and the rays of the moon shone into the room.

The bedroom door was wide open and the patter of feet could be heard as if someone were pacing back and forth through the doorway. The form of a young woman looked carefully into the room. Apparently seeing nobody, she returned on tiptoe to the door and beckoned someone to enter.

Petrified with terror, the men could only look on.

In answer to the beckoning woman, the form of a man entered stealthily and warily and they moved hand in hand towards the table, passing the window as they did so.

Suddenly a phantom arm swept through the air, swinging with terrible force and plunging a knife into the chest of the man who had just entered. Without a sound, the stricken man sunk to the floor, the knife quivering in his chest.

The next moment, a burly form sprang from behind the curtain, seized the young woman and threw her onto the body of her murdered companion. Raising a heavy club, he brought it down with a crushing force on her head.

To the men's horror, a dark stream of blood spread over the phantom forms, the blood of the man mingling with that which flowed from the woman, staining the white floor.

The murderer gazed at his work, wringing his hands. Then, as if overcome with terror, he made a dash for the window, opened it and attempted to get through.

Instinctively, Humphreys raised his revolver and pulled the trigger. The room filled with smoke and the form in the window disappeared. As Humphreys and his companion turned to look at the murdered bodies, they too had vanished.

They called repeatedly to the dog in the darkness but there was no response from the animal. On inspection, their poor companion was found slumped in the corner, stone dead, his eyes lifeless and his neck broken.

Overcome with fright, the men ran out of the house into the open air. With his friend fainting in shock, Humphreys called hoarsely for help to the farmhouses nearby. But he never reached them. After a few steps, he too reeled and fell, overcome with the terrors of the night.

When he recovered consciousness, he found himself in his own room, lying on the floor, convulsively clutching the bedclothes.

CASTELL COCH

TAFF'S WELL

Castell Coch is a 19th century fairy tale castle, situated on the outskirts of Cardiff and famed for its ghostly cavalier. The story comes from reports by the servants of a lady who rented the castle as a private residence from the wealthy Bute family who had rebuilt the castle in a grand gothic style.

Apparently, a male servant told of how he awoke in the middle of the night to find the ghost of a cavalier standing at the foot of his bed. Naturally, the servant had quite a fright but escaped unharmed.

The cavalier is said to have hidden treasure in the walls of the castle before going off to fight in the Civil War. But tragically, he was never to return, except as the ghost apparition who continues searching the castle grounds for what he had lost all those years before.

Another spooky tale associated with the site is of the old Welsh noble, Ifor Bach, said to have owned the original medieval castle that originally stood on the site. Legend has it he used witchcraft to turn two of his men into stone eagles and entrusted them with guarding his treasure which was buried deep within a castle chamber.

Following Ifor Bach's death, two thieves broke into the castle and dug for his great treasure but were foiled by his stone eagles, who instantly sprang to life to fend off the villains. The thieves then met their grisly end. No one has ever discovered Ifor Bach's treasure. Rumour has it the riches remain hidden below the fairy tale castle to this day, waiting to be found.

OYSTERMOUTH CASTLE

2011

The castle which overlooks Swansea Bay at Mumbles is said to be haunted by a whining lady in white, with wounds on her back. The woman, wearing a white robe, has been heard crying in the grounds of the castle on numerous occasions.

Both young children and dogs are reported to have been terrified after seeing her. The ghost is thought to be a servant or a prisoner who was whipped to death at the castle by one of the early Lords of Gower. The castle's whipping post still stands in the castle's large dungeon today.

In one story, a family was picnicking in the grounds of Oystermouth Castle. While the parents rested, their two young children ran off to play. However, the children soon returned to say they'd seen a lady dressed in white crying behind a tree. They led their father to the tree, where he too saw the woman dressed in a long white robe with a cord tied at the waist, seemingly sobbing her heart out, although he heard no sound.

As their dad approached the white lady, he was shocked to see the top part of her dress was ripped to shreds and her back was raw and bleeding from countless lacerations. He stood for a moment then decided to take the children back to his wife. When he returned a few seconds later, there was no sign of the anguished woman in white and it seemed quite impossible for her to have disappeared normally from the scene.

In another story, a local man was taking his dog for a walk near Oystermouth Castle. He lost sight of the dog for some moments and when he whistled and the dog did not return, he began to search for it. After a little while, he heard it whimpering, and he found it behind a tree petrified with fear, its eyes fixed on a part of the castle wall.

It was starting to get dark, but he was curious to know what could have frightened his little dog. He went towards the spot on the castle wall that seemed to have attracted the dog's attention, and as he did so, he saw a white shape on the floor just in front of the wall.

As he got closer the dog began to howl, and the white shape, which he thought may have been a large piece of paper or something similar, rose from the ground. It was a woman dressed in a white robe, and almost before he could recover from his surprise, she seemed to 'melt' into the castle wall.

When he reached the place where she disappeared, he saw that there was no way she could have passed through the wall. As he put it 'the earth just swallowed her up'.

During a conversation between building contractors and a Project Manager near the Castle's Gateway Passage, a figure appeared in the Courtyard and began to walk towards them. Without missing a step, a figure appeared in the courtyard and began to walk towards the village. If it was a ghost, it must have belonged to someone who lived before the walls were built.

The same two contractors also experienced another phenomenon at the same place at 8.30am one morning before any other staff were on-site. They were positioned to the left of the Gateway Passage and not in line of sight of the Gateway entrance. They heard the footsteps of someone walking through the entrance and up the Passageway – since the Castle Gate was locked, they were puzzled and moved to look down the Passageway – but there was nothing to be seen.

In May 2011, a construction worker claims he was tapped on the shoulder while trying to re-open a murder hole. The murder holes at Oystermouth Castle were used by defenders to pour boiling water, oil and even burning, tarred sand down on attacking soldiers. Turning around, the worker saw a vision of a lady in white walking away from him. Catching only a glimpse, he noticed that her face was severely distorted. He needed to be treated at a local doctor's surgery for shock and refused to go back to the site for fear.

On a sunny day in August 2014, a volunteer guide was presenting a short tour of the Castle's ground floor which comprises the Chapel Tower, the South and North Keeps and the Cellars of the West Range. They were about to start the tour when a movement in the north window of the Gatehouse caught the guide's attention: a column of grey smoke was rising within the Portcullis Room. Knowing there was nothing of a flammable nature in this room, the guide just watched. As he did so, the form of a head began to materialise and resolve itself into a female. At this moment, the guide decided to investigate the source of the smoke and quickly made his way to the first floor to find . . nothing . . . the smoke had vanished.

Several years ago, a volunteer was filling a plastic cup with water from the tap at the castle entrance and when the cup was full, it was suddenly knocked out of her hand and fell to the ground. She could not account for what had happened but thought she must have lost her grip without realising it. A few weeks later, the same thing happened, despite her taking extra care when filling the cup. Sometime later, another volunteer wet some kitchen paper at the tap to wipe his face on a hot day. He turned around to walk away and as he stepped forward, the kitchen paper was snatched out of his hand.

Over the past 25 years, several groups and individuals have examined paranormal activities at Oystermouth Castle. The most notable took place at 2am on a cold morning in November 2013. Investigator Geraint Hopkins and his team positioned a camera and tripod in the South Keep where it could be remotely controlled from the Exhibition Tent. At about 2am, all power was lost and the batteries went dead. The electrical system was checked and batteries replaced – the group then discovered that the camera and tripod were not in their original position.

THE GREEN LADY

CAERFFILI CASTLE

Tales abound of hauntings of Caerffili Castle by a lady dressed in green who flits from turret to turret.

The castle's builder, Gilbert de Clare, was married to Princess Alice of Angoulême. When Gruffudd the Fair, Prince of Brithdir, visited the castle, the Welsh prince and princess soon became lovers. Rather stupidly, Gruffudd confessed their secret to a monk, who immediately told Gilbert. Enraged by the treachery, Gruffudd caught the monk and hanged him from a tree at a site now known as Monk's Vale. Maddened with jealousy, Gilbert immediately sent Alice back to France and soon caught up with Gruffudd, hanging him in revenge. He then sent a messenger to inform Alice of her lover's execution. It was such a shock to Alice that she immediately dropped dead.

Her ghost haunts the castle in a dress coloured green to represent Gilbert's envy, hoping to be reunited with her handsome prince.

THE QUEEN'S HEAD PUB

MONMOUTH

The Queen's Head Pub in Monmouth was a frequent resting place for Oliver Cromwell, leader of the Parliamentarians or Round Heads in the English Civil War, who went on to rule the country until 1658. On one occasion during the war, when he was staying at the Queen's Head Hotel, there was an unsuccessful assassination attempt by a Royalist Cavalier who entered the house via a secret passageway in the cellar.

A wall in the old coaching inn relates the tale:

'It is said that when the land was much troubled by civil warr in 1642 secret hiding places be made in the walls of ye Inn – and in ye cellars a passage most secret was dug – hid by a cask half filled – a secret door within, on ye 15 May 1648 Oliver Cromwell was harboured at ye Inn – and that on ye 16 May as he slept a Royalist Cavalier did enter ye Inn through ye secret passage in ye cellare, and did go to Cromwells bed-chamber on intent of murder, but was chased downstairs into the parlour by a Roundhead and shot by the fire.'

There are many reported sightings of ghosts on the premises, including that of a young girl who is frequently spotted roaming the building. Locals tell of a tragic tale of a group of children who were playing near the pub, when a beer barrel broke loose and, rolling down the hill, hit the poor child, killing her instantly.

There have also been sightings of an old man sitting by the fireplace in the bar area, late at night when the pub has closed. Some call him Old Tom, a former owner of the pub who died in the pub and remains there to this day. Old Tom has been known to shout angrily. It may be an idea to leave before last orders are called!

A FAMOUS HAUNTING

THE SKIRRID MOUNTAIN INN

The Skirrid Mountain Inn near Abergavenny is regarded as the oldest public house in Wales and was also used as a courtroom where people were tried and sentenced to death. Justice was swift and more than 180 offenders were hanged from an oak beam over the staircase just outside the courtroom. The markings from the rope can still be seen on the staircase wood today.

These hangings would take place whilst others were downstairs in the inn, drinking ale! Ghostly occurrences in the house include the powerful scent of perfume; glasses flying without being touched; sounds of soldiers in the courtyard, and sightings of the White Lady. Some visitors have also spoken about how they felt a noose being tightened around their neck and marks have remained visible on their necks for days afterwards.

Perhaps spookiest of all took place in the 1990s, during a live radio broadcast from the inn, when a medium sensed a young woman had died of consumption there. No one knew of this event and it was forgotten. However, several months later, a couple researching their family history asked the landlady for information on an ancestor, Harry Price, who had owned the pub in the mid 18th century. They went on to reveal to her that Harry's wife had died of consumption in her early thirties and was buried locally.

MISKIN MANOR

CARDIFF

This 19th century building, now a hotel, was built on a site known to have been occupied at far back as the 10th century.

The most active ghost is that of a lady who regularly appears most nights between midnight and 1am in what is now the bar area. The night porter has long grown accustomed to seeing her and just watches as she drifts from the drawing room to the bar before slowly disappearing into thin air. She is believed to be a former resident of the house and is merely following a path she walked in life. It is known that there used to be a staircase where the bar now stands and it is thought she is climbing that as she gradually disappears.

A team of psychic researchers visited in 2004 but although nothing was seen that night, everyone noticed a sudden change in the atmosphere. Walking down a corridor later, they were bemoaning the lack of psychic activity when suddenly a heavy picture on the wall was thrown onto the floor in front of them.

POWIS CASTLE

WELSHPOOL

Many sightings of ghosts and strange happenings have been reported at Powis Castle, including a mysterious lady in black who can sometimes be seen by the fireside in the Duke's Room. Occasionally, the grand piano in the Ballroom wing can be heard when the room is locked and empty. Other recent sightings include a woman in a mob-cap, a large barking dog and touches from invisible hands.

Perhaps the best-known ghost story associated with Powis Castle took place in 1780. An elderly woman arrived at the castle looking for work as a spinner of hemp and flax. As the Earl was in London, the steward gave her employment and provided her with a bedroom in which to stay. The servants' intentions were to have some fun with the old lady as the room was supposed to be haunted. But they hadn't counted on the woman's resilience.

Later that night, an opulently dressed man, with a gold-lace hat and waistcoat, entered her room three times, walking to the window and leaving the room, closing the door behind him.

On the third visit, she summoned enough courage to ask him what he wanted. When the ghost gestured for her to follow him, she did just that. Directed to a small room, the spirit is said to have lifted one of the floorboards, revealing a locked chest. The ghost then showed her a crevice in the wall where its key was hidden.

'Both must be taken out and sent to the Earl in London,' the ghostly figure ordered her. 'Do this and I will trouble the house no more.'

Upon telling the servants and steward what had happened, she was promised that the ghost's demands would be fulfilled. The Earl was so delighted that he provided for the woman for the rest of her life.

Some say the ghost still visits the room in which the box was found.

GWYDIR CASTLE

LLANWRST

The most significant ghost at Gwydir Castle is that of a young woman who haunts the north wing and the panelled corridor between the Hall of Meredith and the Great Chamber. In the 19th century, the room behind the panelled corridor was called the 'Ghost Room', as an unknown white-haired woman was often spotted roaming the passageway, leaving behind a foul smell of putrefaction. A 1906 account provided a vivid and horrific explanation for the sighting. It is believed that a baronet, Sir John Wynn, seduced a serving maid at Gwydir, and when the relationship became complicated with the girl becoming pregnant, he murdered the girl and had her body stored in the chimney breast . . . a possible explanation for the smell of putrefaction! Interestingly, a few years ago, a hollowed-out space was found within the chimney breast which backs onto the Ghost Room at a spot where the smell is always at its strongest.

During restoration in the 1990s, the new female owner was haunted for months by Lady Margaret, who was married to Sir John Wynn. She triggered a series of 'accidents' apparently intended to harm the new owner's husband. Her good nature darkened radically following the birth of her son in the early 1600s and maybe being married to Sir John was enough to make Lady Margaret hate male owners.

Other sightings include a torchlit procession, crying children and an Elizabethan lady in a yellow dress. Many have reported seeing a ghost dog, a grey wolfhound, and in 1995, dog bones of a similar breed were unearthed in the cellar It has a reputation for being one of the most haunted houses in Wales!

THE GRAVE GUARDIANS

LLANELLI

In Llanelli church yard, the ghost of a white dog used to be seen often. The dog was once owned by a local man from Crickhowell, by the name of Colonel Sandeman.

After the Colonel's death and burial, the loyal dog was often found pining at his master's graveside, refusing to leave, and so, after the dog died, they placed a statue of him on the grave.

Locals started to talk about sinister shadows of the dog seen by passers-by at night. Poachers coming down from the mountain reported their dogs' hackles would rise and the animals would refuse to pass the graveyard.

However, the sight of a single ghost dog is not uncommon in Welsh graveyards. Superstitious lore meant that folk believed that the first person to be buried in a churchyard would be fated to stay earthbound evermore to be the 'Guardian of the Graves'.

This role meant that that soul had the duty to protect all other souls committed to that ground from evil and from trespassers with ill intentions towards the graves. As nobody relished that role, it was often the case that a dog would be buried there instead, for that purpose. The guardian of the graves, therefore, is often sighted as a ghostly spectre of a snarling and fearsome dog, prowling churchyards at night.

A DISTURBING SIGHT

BEDWELLTY

Many 19th century Welsh ghosts have a distinct strangeness about the way they look or move about. Often, they were sighted whirling, throwing stones, walking on their hands or on all fours, whistling and distorting their shapes and terrifying those that witnessed them.

One tale goes that a man by the name of Lewis Thomas was returning from a journey. In passing a field beyond Pont Evan Lliwarch Bridge, on the Bedwellty side of the River Ebbw Fawr, he witnessed a ghost of a man walking on his hands and feet and crossing the path in front of him. It affected him so badly that he never forgot it.

Another tale recounts how, when a John Jenkins hanged himself in a hay loft near Abertillery, his sister discovered his body and let out a scream. Upon hearing the scream, Jeremiah Jones, who lived in a nearby house, looked in her direction, only to see a figure of a man emerging from the hay loft upside down and moving violently towards the direction of the river.

One freakish goblin was sighted by a Thomas Andrew in the parish of Llanhiddel who claimed to have seen a goblin whirling across a wall on all fours, making a horrible mewing sound and shaking its head from side to side.

THE BLACK SHADOWS

GARNLLWYD

In the dark autumn of 1938, one of the oddest ghosts on record drove a family from their home.

David Jones, a colliery foreman, and his wife and sons had recently moved into a cottage on the mountainside at Garnllwyd, South Wales, where they lived for five years without incident.

One day, after the family had returned from a wedding. David's wife asked him if he had noticed anything odd about the bride.

'I was a little surprised by the question,' said the former miner. 'My wife is a very straightforward woman who isn't one to speak of ghosts and such things. On this occasion, however, she was quite struck by something. She was sure she had seen what she described as a shadow floating above the bride's head, something that remained throughout the ceremony. I must admit I saw nothing out of the ordinary but she was adamant that she had seen this eerie shadow.'

A few days later, David came home from work and found his wife unconscious on the floor. She told him, 'I was sleeping. Suddenly I awoke. I could feel something weighing down on the bedclothes, which gradually tightened about me. I put up my hands to ward off some dark shadowy mass which seemed to be enveloping me. Then I collapsed.'

After that, David and his son, also called David, slept in the room and they too had a terrifying experience. Here is David Snr's story.

'Something tugged at the bedclothes. Then I had a feeling that the bedclothes were being drawn tightly around me. I had an awful feeling of being trapped.'

63

His son felt the same eerie influence. They lit a candle but could see nothing, so put the candle out and tried to go back to sleep. David's story goes on.

'Suddenly we knew that it was coming. My body went icy cold. A wave of blackness seemed to be flowing into the room. David shouted, "Get up, Dad, I can see it over your head." '

They put the light on again but could still see nothing. Once dawn arrived, the family abandoned their cottage and moved to Abertillery.

'I'm not sure why this thing entered our home,' stated David, 'but it felt as if it had followed us from the church. Again, why it should have done that, I'm completely in the dark. I'm just pleased we've had no such disturbances since.'

Today, that cottage is empty on the mountain and the curious make pilgrimages to it. But there is no explanation of the weird happenings that drove away the occupants.

Wales seems to be a haunted haven for the phenomenon of spectral black clouds or shadow people. These spectral presences have been the subject of several newspaper reports throughout the late 19th and 20th centuries.

A gentleman from Dyserth in North Wales witnessed a black cloud in the early 1980s.

'I was at my cousin's house in Dyserth which my mother had convinced me was haunted – hanged men in the attic, that kind of thing. She claimed to have seen a man's shadow on top of the lower staircase one night. It was quite a big house, not sure how old. I must have been about six and I was sitting in the dining room at the big wooden table, eating breakfast. My aunt was in the kitchen. I sat eating, happily minding my own business, only to turn my head left at the window to see the most hideous face. It was cloudy like soot, but it had features, though these were wrinkled up, and the face looked like it was melting, like the *Scream* painting. It was very much real.'

THE CHURCHYARD BEAST

WREXHAM 1922

In the last century in Wrexham, there was a house on a slope, looking down across its gardens to a small park and the churchyard two hundred yards away. The house was a rental property, with many guests over the years. Along the front of the house ran a wooden verandah, like an African stoep.

Two brothers and a sister took the house for the summer.

One night, the girl noticed a pinpoint of light moving among the churchyard trees. It flickered to and fro as though someone with a small lantern was walking among the graves. She watched it, wondering idly why anyone should be there so late.

Suddenly the light bobbed up in the air, descended again and moved towards her. Whoever was carrying it had jumped the churchyard wall and was approaching the house. A black misshapen form showed in the moonlight, a hunched form which shambled over the grass.

Stark horror seized her, and she leaped out of bed to bar the windows. They were diamond-paned and heavily leaded. Then she got back into bed. She knew it was in the garden now, coming up the path to the house, a deformed semi-human shape with long trailing arms. An ape, she guessed, escaped from the circus which had visited the village a few days before.

She half thought of calling her brothers and was getting out of bed to do so when suddenly she heard it mounting the steps which led to the verandah. She lay still, breathing hard.

It passed under her window, paused, came back, a moment's silence - and then a hideous face, brown skinned, half-human, with sunken glaring eyes, yellow fangs and high cheekbones, stared in at the window.

The 'thing' fumbled a moment or two, then its fingers scratched at the lead surrounding the window panes. Suddenly a pane fell into the room, and at once, a long, skinny arm was thrust through!

The girl screamed.

More glass was pushed aside, giving the creature space to get in. As it crawled across the floor, her terror was so great that she couldn't even scream as the creature came up to the bed, curled and twisted its spindly fingers in her hair, and pulled her head over the side of the bed, and—.

Fortunately for her, her elder brother, who was awake in the next room, heard her scream and burst in to the rescue, armed with a gun. But the 'thing' was quicker. Her brother just managed to glimpse it, and once he could see that his sister was unharmed, raced out of the house to give chase!

The beast was running down the garden path, with a queer animal gait. The brother fired twice, hitting the creature which spun round, crying thinly, and then limped on again.

It reached the churchyard wall, scrambled over and disappeared among the gravestones. The brother chased him over the wall and could see the beast scuffling into the bushes surrounding a derelict tomb. He ran towards it and found a track like that of an animal leading into the bushes. In the depths of the tangle stood an ancient vault covered with a huge stone catafalque. The ground to one side had been scraped out and a burrow led down into the tomb.

He mounted guard over it, and the butler, who had followed, was sent back for more cartridges. They then kept an all-night vigil over the tomb.

Next morning, the rector, the squire, the local doctor, the chairman of the parish council and the brothers opened the tomb.

Inside was the shrivelled, mummified form of a man, with yellow teeth, and claw-like hands crossed on the breast. It was dead - or seemed so.

'Open the eyelids,' ordered the doctor. Someone lifted one with a match. The eye within was sunken and dead. And then in one leg, the brother saw a bullet hole.

'This "thing" is accursed. It must be burned,' the rector ordered. And there were those there who said that, when this order was given, the dead eye blazed for a moment. The 'thing' was alive.

They took it out from that ghastly tomb and threw it on a great fire in the park.

Y COBLYNAU

The Welsh version of the Cornish Knockers, these gnome-like creatures are said to haunt the mines and quarries of Wales and helped miners by knocking in places with rich lodes of mineral, or metal. Often heard rather than seen, they have been noticed working or lounging round the mine entrances. They dressed in miniature miners' attire and stood at around 18 inches in height. Very ugly to look at with large heads and old men's faces, they are nevertheless often friendly and helpful, often indicating where rich seams of ore or coal exist. It doesn't do to upset them, however, as they have been known to cause rock slides.

The Reverend Edmund Jones of Gwent gives a very interesting account of a version of this habit. One morning William Evans of Hafod-y-Dafel was crossing the Brecon Beacons when he saw an opencast coal mine where none existed. The fairies were cutting coal, filling sacks and loading horses. Lewis Morris, a correspondent of the *Gentleman's Magazine* in 1754, described how, before Esgair y Mwyn lead mine was discovered near Pontrhydfendigaid in Cardiganshire, the local fairies had been seen (and heard) by many people to be hard at work, both day and night. When the mine was established in 1751, they disappeared. The same was also the case at Llwyn Llwyd lead mine near Ysbyty Ystwyth, not far from Esgair y Mwyn. These two cases suggest that the Brecon Beacons vision may well have been an indication of a rich coal seam just beneath the surface.

They will also warn of impending disaster, often by making three distinct knocks against the rock. Generally, then, their presence is welcomed by miners- their noises are not found alarming and it's said to be good luck to see the pixies dancing in a mine entrance.

The sounds made by knockers can be prolonged and are not easily explained by other means. For example, at Llwyn Llwyd, voices, blasting, clearing spoil, levelling roadways, boring, pickaxing and (most notably) pumping were all heard - when there were no pumps working within a mile of the shafts and when, in any case, pumps were very quiet when in operation. Although they may sometimes be heard just once a month or once a year, in 1799 in some mines on Anglesey, the knockers were heard repeatedly over a period of weeks.

Belief in these mine spirits, sometimes thought to be the spirits of dead miners, was once widespread, especially in Celtic areas which were heavily mined, for example Wales and Cornwall. In Germany, these mine spirits were known as Kobolds. It is easy to believe that the dark, cramped, dangerous conditions in a mine would be conducive to supernatural creatures, and other superstitions.

Fairies were often thought to live underground in caves and in crevices.

THE WRECKER

This tragic story is rumoured to have happened in coastal towns all over Wales. An old man and his wife would set false lights, lure ships onto the rocks, and steal their goods.

This tale tells of one night of heavy weather, when, as usual, on hearing a sailing ship was beating in from the west, the pair set their lights and went to bed. The following morning, they headed down to the coast and saw that the ship and most of her crew had died on the rocks that night. The old man could see a man, half dead, rolling in the waves.

The old man took a rock and smashed the sailor over the head, to ensure there were no survivors. But when he turned the body over to search the man's pockets, he found it was his much-loved and only son, a boy who had gone to sea several years before.

WALTER VAUGHAN

AND THE WRECKERS

A more detailed version of this story is to be found near Ogmore in South Wales.

Dunraven Castle was home to the Vaughan family, the last being Walter. As a young man, he was an upstanding member of the community who, it is said, singlehandedly saved many souls shipwrecked off the coast. Walter married and had four children, two of whom drowned in the Channel, while another of his young sons fell into a vat of whey and was drowned.

The tragic loss led Walter to try to set up a sea rescue business but he was refused permission by the governing body of the time. So something in his character changed. He squandered his fortune, his wife died and his only remaining son started a new life abroad.

Years later, a passing ship was wrecked along the Dunraven coast. Close to bankruptcy, Walter, as Lord of the Manor, claimed the spoils for himself and allied himself with a pirate known as Mat of the Iron Hand. When Walter had been a magistrate, he had ordered this wrecker's arrest, during which a scuffle took place, resulting in Mat's hand being amputated and replaced by an iron hook.

Now Mat welcomed Walter and together they organised teams of wreckers to lure ships onto the rocks near Dunraven. On stormy nights, men and women would take lights onto the cliff-tops, causing sailors to think that they were approaching a harbour. Lights were even tied to sheep's tails. Once the ship had grounded, the local wreckers would rush to plunder the rich cargo, jewels and money from dead and half dead mariners and their passengers.

71

One day, Mat sent word to Walter that a galleon was heading up the channel. Rumour had it that it was filled to the brim with tobacco, brandy and gold. It would be perfect for a wrecking.

Walter walked to the headland and saw the vessel straining against the storm. He watched as the galleon broke into pieces, watched as her mast and sails keeled over. He waited to see the lights on the headland move in a steady stream as they were collected by his men as they made their way down to Dunraven Bay.

Not long after dawn, Mat and some of the men lugged vats of brandy and cases of tobacco towards the great house. Walter interrupted his breakfast to assess the loot. Mat had a broad grin on his face and held out a bloodstained sack to Vaughan.

'A special gift for you,' he said.

Vaughan took the bag, expecting some rare jewels to be within. Instead, he found a severed hand. Upon its little finger sat a gold ring bearing the seal of Dunraven - his son's ring.

'An eye for an eye, a tooth for a tooth - his hand for mine,' said Matt of the Iron Hand, watching Walter Vaughan grow pale and crumple to the floor as the full force of his actions and the loss of his last son crashed over him like a wave.

Walter sold Dunraven Castle shortly afterwards and legend has it that he turned mad and died a pauper. Some say that on the anniversary of the galleon's wrecking or perhaps his own death, Vaughan's ghost can be seen walking the headland, looking distressed, shouting silent warnings out to sea.

CAP COCH

OGMORE

In the late 1700s, a pub called the New Inn in Ogmore was a popular spot for anyone wishing to cross the nearby river. The New Inn was owned by Cap Coch, a name given to the landlord by the locals, as he was always seen wearing his red cap. However, no one knew that he was really the leader of a gang of smugglers and outlaws, who often raided and stole from travellers on the local roads. Travellers staying at the New Inn were often at risk of being robbed, or even murdered.

The bodies of victims who paid the ultimate price would on occasion wash up in the river, but Cap Coch was never suspected. Nobody knew about his criminal past until the early 1900s when the New Inn was demolished. A cave was discovered beneath the kitchen, which contained the treasure that he and his gang had stolen.

THE WHITE LADY

OGMORE

The White Lady of Ogmore Castle is a familiar name to many, but her story isn't . . .

The tale tells of a man who was woken in the middle of the night, to see a white lady hovering above him, motioning him to follow her. She led him to ruined Ogmore Castle and told him to lift a stone under which he found a cauldron full of gold. The White Lady told him to take half for himself and to leave the rest where he found them. The man was delighted with his new-found riches, so he took the coins and left the rest, as told, and the white lady disappeared.

The news of the man's mysterious new wealth was the talk of the town, and yet he never revealed his secret. But despite his luxurious new lifestyle, he often thought of the coins he left behind, so one night he crept back to the castle, and found the stone and the rest of the coins.

No sooner had he begun to fill his pockets than a cold chill ran down his spine and the White Lady re-appeared. 'Foolish Man,' she said. 'You have all you could ever need, and yet you still want more. From this night forth, your fortunes shall be reversed.' Her hands turned into claws which she used to scratch the man. Then she vanished.

Very afraid, the man replaced the coins and ran home.

However, in the following weeks, the scratches became septic and despite spending his money on the best doctors around, his condition worsened. Much to his dismay, he revealed the source of his wealth and confessed his foolish second trip to recover the rest of the gold but took the secret of the cauldron's exact location to his grave. His confession led to many people searching the area, in hope they would find the gold, but no one ever has.

YR ADAR LLWCH GWIN

These creatures are said to be very similar to griffins. The name which means 'powdered wine' gives rise to speculation on their colour or possibly the condition of the storyteller!

These birdlike creatures were said to understand human speech and to obey whatever command was given to them by their master.

The story goes that a warrior called Drudwas ap Tryffin was given two Adar Llwch Gwins by his fairy wife.

Drudwas tried to gain advantage in a duel with another man named Arthur by commanding the birds to kill the first fighter to arrive at the duelling ground. This should have been Arthur. Unfortunately, Arthur was late which made Drudwas the first to arrive and his birds, obedient to a fault, tore him to pieces. It must have been a spectacular sight to see.

YR AFANC

The Afanc, sometimes called the Addanc, was a monstrous creature that, like most lake monsters, was said to prey upon anyone foolish enough to fall into or swim in its lake. It has been variously described as a crocodile, beaver, a dwarf-like creature, a platypus or a demon. The lake in which it dwells varies as much as its description.

One tale relates that it was rendered helpless by a maiden who let it sleep upon her lap. While it slept, the maiden's fellow villagers bound the creature in chains. The creature woke up and was understandably furious and its enraged thrashings crushed the maiden, in whose lap it still lay. It was finally dragged away to the lake, Cwm Ffynnon.

Another legend states that its thrashings were so violent that it caused the entire land of Britain to drown. Only two people were saved – Dwyfan and Dwyfach – from whom all later inhabitants of Britain descended.

In yet another version of the tale, the Afanc of the Lake resided in a cave near the 'Palace of the Sons of the King of the Tortures'. The palace is so named because the Afanc slays the three sons (chieftains) of the king each day, only for them to be resurrected by the maidens of the court at night.

No one knows why this cycle of violence continued, but when Peredur (Sir Perceval of the Round Table) asked to ride with the three chieftains who sought out the Afanc daily, they refused to accept his company because, if he were slain, they would not be able to bring him back to life.

So Peredur continued to the cave on his own, wishing to kill the creature and so increase his fame and honour. On his journey, he met a maiden who stated that the Afanc will slay Peredur through cunning, as the beast was invisible and killed his victims with poison darts. The maiden, actually the Queen of Constantinople, gave Peredur an adder stone that would make the creature visible. Peredur ventured into the cave and with the aid of the stone, pierced the Afanc before beheading it.

Snowdonia and its lakes inevitably have versions of this tale. In one, the Afanc lived in Llyn-yr-Afanc in the River Conwy. It was a gigantic beast who, when annoyed, was strong enough to break the banks of the pool causing the floods. Many attempts had been made to kill him but it seems that his hide was so tough that no spear, arrow or any man-made weapon could pierce it.

The wise men of the valley decided that the Afanc must somehow be enticed out of his pool and removed to a lake far away beyond the mountains, where he could cause no further trouble. The lake chosen to be the Afanc's new home was Llyn Ffynnon Las, under the dark imposing shadow of Y Wyddfa.

Preparations started straight away: the finest blacksmith in the land forged the strong iron chains that would be required to bind and secure the Afanc, and they sent for Hu Gardan and his two long-horned oxen – the mightiest oxen in Wales – to come to Betws-y-coed.

They still had to work out how to coax the Afanc out of the lake. Luckily for the villagers, the Afanc was very partial to beautiful young women, and one maiden in particular, the daughter of a local farmer, was brave enough to volunteer for the quest.

The girl approached the Afanc's lake while her father and the rest of the men remained hidden a short distance away. Standing on the shore, she called softly to him. The waters began to heave and churn and through it appeared the huge head of the monster.

Although tempted to turn and run, the girl bravely stood her ground and, gazing fearlessly into the monster's green-black eyes, began to sing a gentle Welsh lullaby.

Slowly the massive great body of the Afanc crawled out of the lake towards the girl. So sweet was the song that the Afanc's head slowly sank to the ground in slumber.

The girl signalled to her father, and he and the rest of the men emerged from their hiding places and set about binding the Afanc with the forged iron chains.

They had only just finished their task when the Afanc awoke, and with a roar of fury at being tricked, slid back into the lake. Fortunately, the chains were long and a few of the men had been quick enough to hitch them onto the oxen, which braced their muscles and began to pull. Slowly, the Afanc was dragged out of the water, but it took the strength of Hu Gardan's oxen and every available man to pull him onto the bank.

They dragged him up the Lledr valley, and then headed north-west toward Llyn Ffynnon Las. On the way up a steep mountain field, one of the oxen was pulling so hard that it lost an eye – it popped out with the strain and the tears the oxen shed formed Pwll Llygad yr Ych.

The mighty oxen struggled on until they reached Llyn Ffynnon Las, close to the summit of Y Wyddfa. There the chains were loosed, and with a roar, the monster leapt straight into the deep blue water that was to become his new home. Encased within the sturdy rock banks of the lake, he remains trapped forever.

THE MORGENS

The Morgen is one of a race of creatures with origins in both Breton and Welsh mythology. They may lure men to their death by their own sylphic beauty, or with glimpses of underwater gardens with buildings of gold or crystal. They are eternally young and like sirens, they sit in the water and comb their hair seductively. They are unique in being able to live and travel between both sea water and freshwater. Accounts exist where Morgens would be adopted by fishermen as infants, only to grow up and leave their adoptive foster-parents behind for their true home under the sea.

Some women are even recorded as having turned into Morgens. Such was the case with Princess Dahut, daughter of Gradlon and Malgven (a Brittanic/Welsh family).

A magician and mischief-maker, Dahut not only caused her family's kingdom of Ys to descend into sin and debauchery, but once, while her father was drunk, she stole his key to the kingdom's dam. As the floodgates burst open and proceeded to sweep the kingdom away, King Gradlon woke up from his slumber, and took off on his magical steed to save her.

Unfortunately, the current of the oncoming waves would prove too strong. It appears Gradlon's efforts would be in vain and Dahut would be carried out to sea, but somehow (by her own magic, or as some divine or infernal punishment for her sinful ways), she transformed into a Morgen.

LLAMHIGYN Y DŴR

'It's winter and Welsh lakes are getting colder than ever. That which lives at the bottom of the biggest lakes, stirs. Stirs, and is very hungry . . .'

So starts a childhood tale, the blood-curdling story of the Llamhigyn y Dŵr, which means 'Water Leaper'.

The Llamhigyn y Dŵr is a most fearsome creature. It is said to have a body resembling a frog but has bat-like wings and a long, tapering tail. But don't think of a cute little frog that could fit in the palm of one hand, nor a huge toad that might be able to fit into a shoebox!

No, the Llamhigyn y Dŵr stands over seven feet tall, and with its tail, measures 15 feet long. It also has a rather nasty 'stinger' on the end of its tail. And its wings? Its wingspan is over 20 feet. They are fast and powerful swimmers, though ungainly on land. Its shriek is enough to turn people mad. When it's hungry, it is said to eat insects, birds and the occasional sheep, using its formidably powerful jaws, and sometimes, just sometimes, it is said to attack people.

It was a great story that used to make me smile, as I had heard it many times before, but it also scared me. As a child, I loved that. Doubly so, because within a few hundred yards of home was a large lake. Could it be home to a Llamhigyn y Dŵr? I never went too close to that lake after dusk, alone, as child.

Anyone who walks past a Welsh lake had better watch for ripples on the lake's surface or listen for any sounds of wings being flapped in the air above. It could be the Llamhigyn y Dŵr, especially if the sun has gone down.

THE GWYBER

Now, the Gwyber (sometimes spelled 'Gwiber') is a most dangerous creature that you would not want to encounter, but if, by chance you did come across one, you should slowly back off, never losing eye-contact.

Gwyber is Welsh for viper or adder, and though those are small snakes, the Gwyber is so much more. It can travel on land or in water, and it can move silently. It eats fish, and when it is really hungry, will slither onto dry land or swoop down from the sky and devour small sheep and other animals.

Although many believe the Gwyber resembles a dragon, the Gwyber is much more like a much-scaled, scarred wyvern, with some having feathered wings. It's really a cross between a long snake and a wyvern, and it stands about seven feet tall (two metres), is green or grey in colour, and is easily camouflaged, virtually unseen. Some say they can actually become invisible.

To make matters even worse, they have long teeth, long, long fangs which drip poisonous venom and which can kill. It can spit that venom, too.

There is a story that, a long time ago, residents of Penmachno near Betws-y-Coed in Conwy, North Wales, the villagers and farmer were being harassed by a Gwyber, a most monstrous beast who devoured the villagers' livestock. So they offered a large sum of money to anyone who could kill the foul beast.

Up stood a young man by the name of Owain ap Gruffydd. Owain, who lived nearby in the mountains, did his research and visited a local wise man called Rhys Ddewin. Rhys told him that his chances of defeating the Gwyber were non-existent, and that he would receive a fatal bite from the creature. Owain left, depressed and greatly worried.

The following day, Owain again visited Rhys Ddewin for advice but this time Owain was dressed as a vagrant. He told the wise man of his plan and Rhys Ddewin again told him that he would lose the battle, fall and suffer a broken neck. Again Owain left, even more depressed and even more worried.

The day after that, Owain went back to the wise man for a third time and enquired again about his chances of killing the creature. Now he was dressed like a miller. Rhys Ddewin freely gave him advice about the Gwyber and concluded that the young miller would die by drowning.

Owain could bear it no more and pulled off his mill worker's disguise, becoming very angry with Rhys Ddewin.

'Three times I've visited you, Rhys Ddewin, and each time you've given me a different prediction regarding my own demise,' Owain shouted.

Rhys Ddewin just smiled sadly and said, 'We will see. Time will tell.'

As a young man, Owain was fearless and maybe a wee bit stubborn. He ran out of Rhys Ddewin's cottage at Penmachno and set off down the valley in search of the Gwyber to kill it.

The valley was steep indeed, and as Owain was striding across some rocks, the Gwyber struck, swooping down from the sky, flapping its tremendous wings. Without warning, the Gwyber bit poor Owain on the neck. Owain fought back bravely and lashed out wildly with his sword. So wildly that he slipped on the rocks. He fell awkwardly, with such force that he hit his head and he heard the most gruesome snap like a branch breaking, as his neck broke. Owain rolled on those slippery rocks and fell into the deep, fast-flowing river at the foot of the valley and drowned.

When Owain's lifeless body was discovered by his friends, they set off to kill the Gwyber. After several hours of searching, they found the Gwyber on the bank of the river, wounded, bloodied, exhausted, half-dead, thanks to Owain's battle with it, but not quite dead. With a blood-curdling scream, the Gwyber lunged at them. They each let loose a hail of arrows, and the creature fell backwards, plunged into the river and was never, ever seen again.

The people of Penmachno were pleased that Owain and his friends, by working together, had killed the creature, but were saddened that the good fight had come at an enormous cost to dear Owain.

Even to this day, it is said the people of Penmachno rarely venture alone into the nearby national park at dusk – Gwydir National Park – for fear of encountering the Gwyber.

CWRGI GARWLWYD

Cwrgi Garwlwyd is a legendary warrior, sometimes also described as being a werewolf. Gwrgi was one of King Arthur's warriors, who fought against various monsters and people. He was such a prolific killer that he became a menace, killing one Briton a day.

However, Gwrgi maintained his piety and would kill two men on a Saturday to avoid killing any man on a Sunday. He was eventually killed by a bard and his death was seen as a great fortune.

THE BLUE ROOM

ABERGLASNY HOUSE

The house and grounds of Aberglasney House are reported to be haunted. Thomas Phillips, a wealthy surgeon with the East India Company, who owned the property and died in 1824, has reportedly been seen by gardeners and butlers on many occasions in the grounds.

After Phillips's death, bad luck affected the house's successive owners, and many children died in their infancy at the house. Pigeon House Wood at the rear of the property is said to be one of the many paranormal hotspots in the area. Many visitors, on reaching a certain point in the woods, report feeling a sudden fear, followed by an eerie coldness. In 1999, a medium visited this area and claimed that a fugitive had spent his last moments here, trying to evade capture. However, he was captured and shot and it's his emotions before his death that are felt by people in the vicinity.

According to an Aberglasney tradition dating back to the time of the Rudds who owned the house from about 1600, disembodied candle-flames, or corpse candles, appear to foretell a death. The number of flames corresponds with the numbers of deaths. When a housekeeper in the 1630s saw five lights in a room, following some redecoration or building work, five maidservants were found to have died overnight. The tale comes in varying versions. Sometimes the number of maids is different, and sometimes rather than death by suffocation (from coal fumes, presumably), the maids die from arsenic poisoning, present in the wallpaper of the newly redecorated Blue Room.

THE PHYSICIANS OF MYDDFAI

CARMARTHENSHIRE

High up in a hollow of the Black Mountains of South Wales is a lonely sheet of water called Llyn y Fan Fach.

In a farm not far from this lake, there lived in olden times a widow, with an only son whose name was Gwyn. When this son grew up, he was often sent by his mother to look after the cattle grazing. The place where the sweetest food was to be found was near the lake, and it was there that the mild-eyed beasts wandered whenever they wanted to. One day, when Gwyn was walking along the banks of the mere, watching the kine cropping the short grass, he was astonished to see a lady standing in the clear smooth water, some distance from the land.

She was the most beautiful creature that he had ever set eyes upon, and she was combing her long hair with a golden comb, the unruffled surface of the lake serving her as a mirror.

He stood on the brink, gazing fixedly at the maiden, and straightway knew that he loved her. As he gazed, he unconsciously held out to her the barley-bread and cheese which his mother had given him before he left home. The lady gradually glided towards him, but shook her head as he continued to hold out his hand, saying,

'Cras dy fara, O thou of the crimped bread, Nid hawdd fy nala, It is not easy to catch me.'

She dived under the water and disappeared from his sight.

He went home, full of sorrow, and told his mother of the beautiful vision which he had seen. As they pondered over the strange words used by the mysterious lady before she plunged out of sight, they concluded that there must have been some spell connected with the hard-baked bread, and the mother advised her son to take with him some 'toes', or unbaked dough, when next he went to the lake.

Next morning, long before the sun appeared above the crest of the mountain, Gwyn was by the lake with the dough in his hand, anxiously waiting for the Lady of the Lake to appear above the surface. The sun rose, scattering with its powerful beams the mists which veiled the high ridges around, and mounting high in the heavens.

Hour after hour, the youth watched the waters, but hour after hour, there was nothing to be seen except the ripples raised by the breeze and the sunbeams dancing upon them. By the late afternoon, despair had crept over the watcher, and he was on the point of turning his footsteps homeward when, to his intense delight, the lady again appeared above the sunlit ripples. She seemed even more beautiful than before, and Gwyn, forgetting in admiration of her fairness all that he had carefully prepared to say, could only hold out his hand, offering to her the dough. She refused the gift with a shake of the head as before, adding the words,

'Llaith dy fara, O thou of the moist bread, Ti ni fynna, I will not have thee.'

Then she vanished under the water, but before she sank out of sight, she smiled upon the youth so sweetly and so graciously that his heart became fuller than ever with love. As he walked home slowly and sadly, the remembrance of her smile consoled him and awakened the hope that when next she appeared, she would not refuse his gift. He told his mother what had happened, and she advised him that, because the lady had refused both hard-baked and unbaked bread, to take with him next time bread that was half-baked.

That night, he did not sleep a wink, and long before the first dawn rays, he was walking the margin of the lake with half-baked bread in his hand, watching its smooth surface even more impatiently than the day before.

The sun rose and the rain came, but the youth heeded nothing as he eagerly strained his gaze over the water.

Morning wore to afternoon, and afternoon to evening, but nothing met the eyes of the anxious watcher but the waves and the myriad dimples made in them by the rain.

The shades of night began to fall, and Gwyn was about to depart in sore disappointment, when, casting a last farewell look over the lake, he beheld some cows walking on its surface. The sight of these beasts made him hope that they would be followed by the Lady of the Lake, and, sure enough, before long, the maiden emerged from the water. She seemed lovelier than ever, and Gwyn was almost beside himself with joy at her appearance. His rapture increased when he saw that she was gradually approaching the land, and he rushed into the water to meet her, holding out the half-baked bread in his hand. She, smiling, took his gift, and allowed him to lead her to dry land. Her beauty dazzled him, and for some time, he could do nothing but gaze upon her. And as he gazed upon her, he saw that the sandal on her right foot was tied in a peculiar manner. She smiled so graciously upon him that he at last recovered his speech and said, 'Lady, I love you more than all the world besides and want you to be my wife.'

She would not consent at first. However, he pleaded so earnestly that she at last promised to be his bride, but only on the following condition.

'I will wed you,' she said, 'and I will live with you until I receive from you three blows without a cause - tri ergyd diachos. When you strike me the third causeless blow, I will leave you for ever.'

He was protesting that he would rather cut off his hand than employ it in such a way, when she suddenly darted from him and dived into the lake. His grief and disappointment were so sore that he determined to put an end to his life by casting himself headlong into the deepest water of the lake. He rushed to the top of a great rock overhanging the water and was on the point of jumping in when he heard a loud voice saying, 'Forbear, rash youth, and come hither.'

He turned and saw on the shore of the lake, some distance from the rock, a hoary-headed old man of majestic mien, accompanied by two maidens. He descended from the rock in fear and trembling, and the old man addressed him in comforting accents.

'Mortal, thou wishest to wed one of these my daughters. I will consent to the union if thou wilt point out to me the one thou lovest.'

Gwyn gazed upon the two maidens, but they were so exactly similar in stature, apparel and beauty that he could not see the slightest difference between them. They were such perfect counterparts of each other that it seemed quite impossible to say which of them had promised to be his bride, and the thought that, if perchance he fixed upon the wrong one, all would be for ever lost, nearly drove him to distraction. He was almost giving up the task in despair when one of the two maidens very quietly thrust her foot slightly forward. The motion, simple as it was, did not escape the attention of the youth, and looking down he saw the peculiar shoe-tie which he had observed on the sandal of the maiden who had accepted his half-baked bread. He went forward and boldly took hold of her hand.

'Thou hast chosen rightly,' said the old man. 'Be to her a kind and loving husband, and I will give her as a dowry as many sheep, cattle; goats, swine and horses as she can count of each without drawing in her breath. But remember, if thou strikest her three causeless blows, she shall return to me.'

Gwyn was overjoyed, and again protested that he would rather lop off all his limbs than do such a thing. The old man smiled and, turning to his daughter, desired her to count the number of sheep she wished to have. She began to count by fives - one, two, three, four, five - one, two, three, four, five - one, two, three, four, five - as many times as she could until her breath was exhausted. In an instant as many sheep as she had counted emerged from the water. Then the father asked her to count the cattle she desired. One, two, three, four, five - one, two, three, four, five - one, two, three, four, five - she went on counting until she had to draw in her breath again.

Without delay, black cattle to the number she had been able to reach came lowing out of the mere. In the same way, she counted the goats, swine and horses she wanted, and the full tally of each kind ranged themselves alongside the sheep and cattle. Then the old man and his other daughter vanished.

The Lady of the Lake and Gwyn were married amid great rejoicing and took up their home at a farm named Esgair Llaethdy, where they lived for many years. They were as happy as happy can be, everything prospered with them, and three sons were born to them.

When the eldest boy was seven years old, there was a wedding some distance away, to which Nelferch - for that was the name the Lady of the Lake gave herself - and her husband were specially invited. When the day came, the two began walking through a field in which some of their horses were grazing, when Nelferch said that the distance was too great for her to walk and she would rather not go.

'We must go,' said her husband, 'and if you do not like to walk, you can ride one of these horses. Do you catch one of them while I go back to the house for the saddle and bridle.'

'I will,' she said. 'At the same time, bring me my gloves. I have forgotten them - they are on the table.'

He went back to the house, and when he returned with the saddle, bridle and gloves, he found to his surprise that she had not stirred from the spot where he had left her. Pointing to the horses, he playfully flicked her with the gloves and said, 'Go, go (dos, dos).'

'This is the first causeless blow,' she said with a sigh, and reminded him of the condition upon which she had married him, a condition which he had almost forgotten.

Many years after, they were both at a christening. When all the guests were full of mirth and hilarity, Nelferch suddenly burst into tears and sobbed piteously. Gwyn tapped her on the shoulder and asked her why she wept. 'I weep,' she said, 'because this poor innocent babe is so weak and frail that it will have no joy in this world. Pain and suffering will fill all the days of its brief stay on earth, and in the agony of torture will it depart this life. And, husband, thou hast struck me the second causeless blow.'

After this, Gwyn was on his guard, day and night, not to do anything which could be regarded as a breach of their marriage covenant. He was so happy in the love of Nelferch and his children that he knew his heart would break if, through some accident, he gave the last blow which would take his dear wife from him.

Some time after, the babe whose christening they had attended, after a short life of pain and suffering, died in agony, as Nelferch had foretold. Gwyn and the Lady of the Lake went to the funeral, and amid the mourning and grief, Nelferch laughed merrily, causing all to stare at her in astonishment. Her husband was so shocked at her high spirits on so sad an occasion, that he touched her, saying, 'Hush, wife, why dost thou laugh?'

'I laugh,' she replied, 'because the poor babe is at last happy and free from pain and suffering.' Then rising, she said, 'The last blow has been struck. Farewell.'

She started off immediately towards Esgair Llaethdy, and when she arrived home, she called her cattle and other stock together, each by name. The cattle she called thus,

Mu wlfrech, moelfrech, Brindled cow, bold freckled,
Mu olfrech, gwynfrech, Spotted cow, white speckled;
Pedair cae tonn-frech, Ye four field sward mottled.
Yr hen wynebwen, The old white-faced,
A'r las Geigen, And the grey Geigen
Gyda'r tarw gwyn, With the white bull
O llys y Brenin, From the court of the King,
A'r llo du bach, And thou little black calf,

91

Sydd ar y bach, Suspended on the hook,

Dere dithe, yn iach adre! Come thou also, whole again, home.

They all immediately obeyed the summons of their mistress. The little black calf, although it had been killed, came to life again, and descending from the hook, walked off with the rest of the cattle, sheep, goats, swine and horses at the command of the Lady of the Lake.

It was the spring of the year, and there were four oxen ploughing in one of the fields. To these she cried,

Y pedwar eidion glas, Ye four grey oxen,

Sydd ar y maes, That are on the field,

Deuwch chwithe, Come you also

Yn iach adre! Whole and well home!

Away went the whole of the livestock with the Lady across the mountain to the lake from whence they had come and disappeared beneath its waters. The only trace they left was the furrow made by the plough which the oxen drew after them into the lake. This remains to this day.

Gwyn's heart was broken. He followed his wife to the lake, crushed with woe, and put an end to his misery by plunging into the cold water. The three sons distracted with grief, almost followed their father's example, and spent most of their days wandering about the lake in the hope of seeing their lost mother once more. Their love was at last rewarded, for one day Nelferch appeared suddenly to them.

She told them that their mission on earth was to relieve the pain and misery of mankind. She took them to a place which is still called the Physician's Dingle (Pant y Meddygon), where she showed them the virtues of the plants and herbs which grew there and taught them the art of healing.

Profiting by their mother's instruction, they became the most skilful physicians in the land. Rhys Grug, Lord of Llandovery and Dinefwr Castles, gave them rank, lands and privileges at Myddfai for their maintenance in the practice of their art and for the healing and benefit of those who should seek their help. The fame of the Physicians of Myddfai was established over the whole of Wales and continued for centuries among their descendants.

The Physicians of Myddfai were actually herbalists in the twelfth century, which was a time of influx of new ideas and learning that inspired and gave momentum to the Gothic era. Contrary to the prevalent view that the medieval times were a time of darkness, it was in fact a period of immense cultural importance, with the first universities being founded and monastic schools established. A range of new knowledge became available through translation, including medical texts.

Myddfai was one such centre that flowered because of this new knowledge. In about 1177 AD, the Welsh prince Lord Rhys (1132-1197), ruler of the kingdom of Deheubarth in South Wales, was instrumental in sponsoring the monasteries of Talley and Strata Florida. As the name of the latter - meaning 'Layers of Flowers' - suggests, these abbeys also flourished as schools and hospitals of herbal medicine.

Rhiwallon, who was the most able practitioner in the area, became the eminent personal physician to Lord Rhys at Dinefwr. Rhiwallon was assisted by his three sons, Cadwgan, Griffith and Einon. In return, they were rewarded with land around Myddfai.

'Lord Rhys maintained their rights and privileges in all integrity and honour was met.'

It is at these monasteries that the Physicians of Myddfai would have acquired a lot of their practical skills of herbal medicine. The scholasticism of the monks too would have encouraged writing their recipes down. This they did, 'as a record of their skill lest no one should be found with the skill they were'. However, 'it is unlikely that their materia medica came from that era.' Most likely it was an

93

accumulation of knowledge from the preceding centuries of herbal usage by the tribes and villages of South Wales.

PRINCESS GWENLLIAN

THE GOWER

1135 was the start of a time of turbulence throughout England and Wales. Henry I had designated his daughter Matilda as the next ruler, a decision challenged after Henry's death by Stephen of Blois. The resultant war encouraged Welsh rulers to challenge their Norman overlords and reclaim their rightful heritage. In 1136, the Welsh won a surprising victory at the Battle of Llwchwr in which around 500 Normans were killed. Hoping to dispel the Normans from all of Wales, Gruffydd ap Rhys (c.1090-1137), who ruled Deheubarth in South Wales, travelled north to plot with his father-in-law, Gruffudd ap Cynan, the ruler of Gwynedd, thinking this was their opportunity to expel the Normans from the Welsh kingdoms.

In his absence, the Norman Lord of Kidwelly, Maurice de Londres, launched a counterattack. Gwenllian, Gruffydd's wife, learning that the Normans were heading towards them in great numbers, quickly marshalled an army which sadly was small and ill-equipped. She chose instead to wage a guerilla war and divided her army, sending some to attack the Norman ships under the command of a neighbour, Gruffydd ap Llewellyn. The rest of her forces would attack the Normans' supply lines around Kidwelly. Sadly for Gwenllian and the Welsh, Gruffydd ap Llewellyn betrayed her to the Normans and a pitched battle became inevitable. One of her sons, Morgan, was killed trying to protect his mother, and another, Maelgwyn, captured. Gwenllian was captured and then beheaded at what is now Maes Gwenllian. Legend has it that Gwenllian's headless ghost roams Maes Gwenllian and the town of Kidwelly, perhaps searching for her head.

TEGGIE

Does North Wales have its very own version of the Loch Ness Monster?

Llyn Tegid in Bala is the largest lake in Wales and abounds with ghostly phenomena. At four miles long, half a mile wide and more than 140 feet deep, it is home to the Gwyniad fish which have lived there for the past 10,000 years or more, a relic of the last Ice Age. Although they are too small to be mistaken for a monster, the lake is large and deep enough to hide any much bigger species still surviving in the depths.

What is now the lake was once the legendary home to the court of Tegid Foel, the giant husband of the sorceress Ceridwen. The court is now hidden beneath the waters of the lake after being suddenly drowned. Locals report seeing court lanterns shimmering underwater on moonlit nights.

Since the 1920s, reports have cropped up periodically of a creature emerging from the depths of Llyn Tegid to terrify and intrigue bystanders. Described as greyish brown or black, and typically between 8-12 feet long, it is believed to have one or two humps, a long neck and a round football-sized head with a crocodilian snout. Some have also described the figure as a small dinosaur.

Like the fabled Nessie of Loch Ness in Scotland, the monster has even been given its own nickname - Teggie.

One of the most notable reported sightings of Teggie was by former lake manager Dewi Bowen in the 1970s.

Mr Bowen is reported to have said, 'I was looking out at the lake and saw this thing coming towards the shore. It was at least 8ft long, similar to a crocodile, with its front and rear ends about 4ins above the water.' However, after rushing closer to the water to investigate, he found nothing.

One alleged witness in 1979 claimed to have seen the surface foam and bubble and a large hump-backed beast emerge. In 1992, a female visitor to the lake reported her close encounter.

'It was twilight and I was on the shingle beach of the lake. Feeling I was being watched, I suddenly turned a full 180 degrees and found I was staring straight at the monster. It was about 60 feet away, its black head and neck clear above the surface of the water.'

In 2006, Rhodri Jones whose sheep farm extends to the lake's foreshore reported seeing a crocodile-sized creature moving through the waters on a still night. Neighbouring farmers have also reported such sightings.

Other claims have emerged over the years that Teggie has been spotted by fishermen and visitors to the lake.

So can there really be a monster lurking beneath in the depths of Llyn Tegid?

Other legends surround Llyn Tegid. In 1607, a young farmer went missing whilst walking by the lake mourning the death of his beloved wife. Villagers assumed he had killed himself by drowning but 15 years later, he reappeared in exactly the same spot. Everyone was stunned to find he had not aged at all and had developed the ability to play the flute. He was never able to account for the missing years.

In 1743, in the middle of a July heatwave, villagers were amazed to find the surrounding mountains were covered in snow and icicles. Hundreds of fish lay on the shore, twitching for hours before they died. The snow lasted for three more days before eventually thawing.

GWRACH Y RHIBYN

Translated as the Witch of Rhibyn or the Hag of the Dribble, the Gwrach y Rhibyn is a Welsh spirit who appears to families of pure Welsh blood to warn them that death is fast approaching. Something of a cross between a fairy, a warning and a vampire and often compared to an Irish banshee, the Gwrach y Rhibyn takes on a hideous appearance. She often appears as quite ugly with a crooked back, long, black, knotted hair, black teeth, bone-thin legs, a pallid complexion, and, in some cases, leather wings. The most frightfully inhuman of all her features, however, are her long thin arms, for not only do they end in dreadful talon-like hands, but black scaly wings also hang from these extremities. These bat-like appendages are thought capable of flight. What clothing she does wear is black and ragged. Sometimes one of her eyes is grey, the other black but they are always deeply sunken and piercing. Often, she is accompanied by a great black hound, known as Gwyllgi, the Dog of Darkness.

Many stories of the Gwrach y Rhibyn seem to place her in or near a water source and she seems particularly to enjoy suddenly leaping and scaring the victim. Other times, she will silently stalk her victims. They may feel a tingle or as if they're being watched but the Gwrach y Rhibyn will not reveal herself until they pass a water channel or a crossroads.

When the victim is finally able to lock eyes with her, she presents herself in all her horrible glory and shrieks. The person who sees the ghost is being warned of their imminent death, or the imminent death of someone close to them. Once the Gwrach y Rhibyn has revealed herself, she utters one of a few different cries. For example, if the person who is going to die is a man, she yells, 'Fy ngwr! Fy ngwr! (which translates to *My husband! My husband*). Or, if the soon-to-be-deceased is a child, she'll yell, 'Fy mlentyn! Fy mlentyn bach!' (which translates to *My child! My little child!*)

In addition to being a frightening harbinger of impending death, she also has other elements that make her even more frightening. Despite her misleading calls seeming to mourn a child who is about to die, it is said she actually enjoys capturing and drinking their blood. She never kills the children, though. Instead, she terrifies them and takes a fair amount of their blood, leaving them to find their way home alone. They often appear pale and sickly when they finally do arrive home. It seems she may even feed on the blood of babies by directly visiting them in their cribs. If a babe was healthy and strong when it was first born but grows to become more sickly and pale, it is said that the Gwrach y Rhibyn must be feasting on it.

The blood stains her teeth black and adds to her horrendous appearance. Some descriptions of her also note that her mouth is caked in blood or that she has one particularly long, hollow tooth that she uses to drink the blood of the children.

Like small children and babies who are often defenceless, it was also said that she would drink the blood of the old and bedridden because they could not stop her advances.

Although strong, Gwrach y Rhibyn can be fought off with physical force. The only other way to ward her off or remove her from feasting on another human is to utter the Name of God or wave a crucifix in her direction.

Few tales exist of those who encountered this witch, maybe because they didn't live long enough to reveal the meeting, possibly dying of shock at the vision!

One such meeting happened in November 1877. While visiting an old friend in Llandaff, a farmer was sleeping soundly in his bed when he was abruptly awakened 'by a terrible screeching and shaking of the window. It was a loud and clear screech, and the shaking of my window was very plain, but it seemed to go by like the wind.' Excited more than frightened, the farmer jumped out of bed, ran over to the window, and flung the thing open. What he saw next would haunt him for the rest of his life . . .

'Then I saw the Gwrach Y Rhibyn,' the farmer said, 'a horrible old woman with long red hair and a face like chalk, and great teeth like tusks, looking back over her shoulder at me as she went through the air with a long black gown trailing along the ground below her arms, for body I could make out none.' The hag gave out another ungodly shriek while the farmer stared at her, completely dumbfounded. Then he heard the creature buffeting her wings against another window on a house just below the one he was staying in before finally vanishing from his sight. The farmer stared into the night and swore that 'as I am a living man, sir, I saw her go in at the door of the Cow and Snuffers Inn, and return no more.' He watched the inn's door for a long time after the incident, but he never saw her come back out before he drifted off into sleep once again.

The next day, the farmer was told that the innkeeper of the Cow and Snuffers, a man called Llewellyn, had died in the night. The man had kept the inn for seventy years, and his family for three hundred years before him, at the exact same inn. The farmer, having sworn that all of this was true, left his audience with one last thought: 'It's not these new families that the Gwrach Y Rhibyn ever troubles, it's the old stock'. From the sound of it, the farmer was lucky to be alive after his encounter! It seems that, on that particular night, the Gwrach Y Rhibyn had only come to warn of an approaching death. Needless to say, they got lucky.

The next recorded instance of an encounter with the Gwrach Y Rhibyn comes from Dr Bob Curran, from his book *Vampires* (2005). In the hamlet of Llyn-y-Guelan-Goch, near Llanfor, lived a retired Christian minister by the name of Reverend Elias Pugh. He was well-liked by the locals and was said to be both saintly and a man of great faith. He also knew a great deal about witchcraft and how to combat those dark forces. It was even rumoured that he had exorcised and banished ghosts from a home at one time. An ancient burial ground was situated close to the village with a very evil reputation. People going past the place's crumbling walls claimed to have seen ghost lights flying about the outer walls and reported hearing dreadful sounds from beneath the ground. Needless to say, the villagers were deeply afraid of the place, and avoided going anywhere near it, especially after dark. But they had never had a serious incident, until late one night . . .

This particular night, an elderly woman by the name of Ann Hughes was walking by the old cemetery. Peering into the darkness, she saw a dark, stooping figure wandering through the weathered gravestones. It appeared to be another old woman like herself, but Ann knew it was unlikely to be anyone local as they would never dare enter the graveyard at night. The figure was moving too quickly for her to see who it might be, and then it vanished. Although there was a full moon, she couldn't see anything else, so she simply shrugged her shoulders and moved on.

Before too long, Ann began feeling that something was following her. Crippled by arthritis, Ann could only move slowly but the thing seemed content to walk at her pace. She made a pained effort to hurry along, not daring to look around out of fear of what might be there. In a short time, a crossroads appeared, and the thing behind her began moving faster. Ann glanced behind her, only to see a bluish-white flame the size of a man rushing towards her! The flame suddenly began to change, condensing itself into the form of an old lady, which 'looked like a Hag in an old green cloak, down the front of which were dribbles of red – perhaps of blood!' Mrs Hughes tried to fight the hideous thing off, but it was too powerful! Ann eventually passed out and fell down on the road.

When Mrs Hughes awoke, she found herself lying on the road, all alone. Feeling a pain on her wrist, she was horrified to find a small, bleeding puncture wound. She knew that this was where the monster had been drinking her blood. Carefully picking herself up, Ann quickly made her way home and bolted the door shut behind her. For much of the night, Ann 'thought that she heard the Gwrach Y Rhibyn moving and scraping about outside her house, trying to get in'. When dawn finally came, Mrs Hughes believed that it was finally over.

Over the next two months, many people became sick, and several died. Meanwhile, the hideous hag-creature was seen many times near the crumbling graveyard. Knowing what the creature was, the villagers agreed something had to be done. So, a group of them, including Ann Hughes, asked the Reverend Elias Pugh to do something about the visitations. The Reverend knew 'that the cemetery held some people of somewhat dubious repute' and believed that the people buried there may have indeed been what had brought the hag into the area to begin with. But the man also knew that once she had tasted a community's blood, it would be very difficult to drive the Gwrach Y Rhibyn away for good. Elias wasn't a violent man but he knew the only way to get rid of the hag's presence was with physical violence, and thus would have to be quite literally beaten out. He carved a stout, heavy stick for himself to use as a weapon, and made his way to the cemetery.

Night had fallen, and the moon was full and bright when the Reverend reached the burial ground. For an instant, he saw a sphere of light weaving and bobbing through the old headstones, just beyond the ruined wall. As he drew closer, he saw a figure crouching down in the darkness. It was wearing a tattered green gown, 'from which a pale light – the glow of putrescence – flickered'. Gripping his cudgel tighter, the Reverend moved closer. Suddenly, the figure turned into a ball of light and darted towards him! When the light reached Pugh, it assumed a humanlike shape and knocked him to the ground. The priest lashed out with his staff, and it hit something solid. The thing sounded hollow, 'as if he had struck an empty drum'. The blow knocked the creature back, but then it jumped at him again! Pugh looked up and saw 'a greasy green head-covering and, below it, almost solid darkness. The thing had no face!' He also saw that upon the front of the creature's clothing were several reddish-brown streaks. Those streaks couldn't have been anything but dried blood! At that moment, the Reverend Pugh realised that this demonic creature was none other than the notorious Gwrach Y Rhibyn, and Elias knew that he was going to die unless he did something immediately!

In an instant, he knew what to do. 'In the Name of God, leave me be!' the Reverend shouted. The weight on his chest disappeared, and the creature retreated. The Reverend Pugh knew at that moment that it was his faith that had saved him from certain death. But he needed to get back home, and hurriedly made his way back to the house. Once home, the Reverend immediately began preparing for his next battle with the hag. Elias started by cutting himself another heavy stick, but this time he carved a small cross into the head of the cudgel. With the moon still full, he returned to the cemetery the very next night.

Sure enough, Pugh saw the orb of light flying around the ancient headstones again. He began moving towards the low wall, and the light once again approached him. The light slowly took on the form of the hideous old hag, and she shot out her long, black tongue at the priest. Raising his staff, Pugh dealt it a hard blow, and the hag quickly retracted her tongue. But she kept advancing on him, and each time he struck her, she got back up and kept coming. The hag stood up and towered over him, and she opened her mouth far wider than was possible. The Reverend had had enough. Grasping his cudgel with both hands, he struck the hag so hard that it sent her reeling to the ground! Pugh started walking towards her, and suddenly the Gwrach Y Rhibyn 'turned into a ball of light, almost as big as a man, and shot off across the nightbound country. It wasn't seen in that area again.'

THE BANSHEE OF MYNYDD MEIO SHINNEY

'If this mountain could speak, there'd be no sleep.' The mountains near Abertridwr, in particular Mynydd Meio, have been housing, sheltering, looking down upon a community for millennia.

The stories of Shinney date back four thousand years and are attached to a Neolithic burial site on the mountain which contained the remains of over 40 half-burnt and painted bodies. She is the banshee, the guardian of entrances to the other world and the shepherd of men. She can identify men of mixed blood. They will not know this, though they may have, at times, an affinity with other worldly things which puzzles them. Shinney will try to lure them to the top of Mynydd Meio and for this, she has three guises. She can be aged and decrepit in need of assistance, young and pathetic, lost alone, beautiful and alluring, offering excitement and danger, or she can be all of these things.

The road up out of the Taff Valley onto Mynydd Meio is still called 'Heol y Bunshee' - The Banshee Road. It is an ancient drovers' track that passes the ruined isolation hospital below the burial sites of Mynydd Meio as it winds its way to the hidden sanctuary of the mountain church.

The banshee waits on the road. She waits at a ford, a ford she uses to wash the heads, the heads she tirelessly collects. The story is a remnant of the old religion. The banshee's lures have been painted over a hundred times. If you stood up there alone, you'd love the mountain too, but it's better if it doesn't love you back.

Children in the area grew up with tales of Shinny but she was called Spinning Mary. If they saw dead sheep bones, they would say that Spinning Maru had killed and eaten them.

A GHOST STORY

CWMYNYSCOY

One ghostly place is the Glyn Ponds, just off the Pontypool to Crumlin road. About 1880, the hero of this story, old Henry Jones, was living in one of the cottages on the Priscoch ridge overlooking Cwmynyscoy. At work one day in the mines, he saw a ghost, dressed an ancient and outlandish fashion, who commanded him to meet it at a certain hour on the following night at a place on the mountain, somewhere in the direction of Crumlin. It was a long distance from the Cwm to this spot, it was not very pleasant travelling after nightfall, and a ghost was not so attractive, so Henry did not go.

But the ghost incessantly persecuted him. It was with him in the mine. It accompanied him in his walks, no matter who was with him.

'There it is,' he would exclaim.

'Where?' asked his companions, feeling a thrill of horror shoot through them.

'There,' he said, pointing with his finger.

'We see nothing there.'

'But it is there, close to you!'

On hearing this, his friends quickly left a clear space in the direction indicated, their hair standing on their heads as they looked that way. Even when he was in bed with his wife, he was not permitted to rest, for the ghost came and pulled the clothes off them!

The haunted man could stand it no longer and gave his solemn promise that if the ghost would come to the Cwm on a certain night and fetch him, he would accompany it wherever it liked to take him. He made no secret of the arrangement. His friends became alarmed for his safety and declared that he should not budge an inch but he was resolute. The night came, and the inhabitants of the Cwm mustered in strong force and got him in their midst to prevent his being carried away. Even a prayer meeting was held!

All at once it was discovered that he was missing, taken away out of the very middle of the crowd! And many swore that they saw him walking up and up in the air till he was lost to sight in the darkness.

The story goes that, after being lifted to a great height, he was carried off across the country. Far below him, he saw the fires blazing out at the Blaendare furnaces; far below him, as he swept onwards, the waters of the Glyn, faintly gleaming in the pitch-dark hollow as it reflected the few stars that twinkled in the moonless sky and by and by, he alighted on the mountain side. Not far from him stood a solitary tree, to the foot of which the ghost led him.

'Remove those stones' said the ghost, pointing to a little heap, 'and dig with your hands.'

The man did as he was bid, and presently grabbed out a great bar of gold.

'Take it up, and bring it quickly along,' said the ghost. Immediately afterwards, they were soaring through the air on the return journey. Back they flew, till they hovered over the centre of the Glyn Pond.

'Now drop the gold,' the ghost commanded.

Henry let it fall and heard the splash as it sank deep in the water below.

'At last,' cried the spirit, with a great sigh of relief. 'I shall now find rest at last!'

One other 'true' version related that the ghost brought the treasure with him to the Cwm and Jones and his queer comrade sat and rested upon it (!) in mid-air before they dropped it into the Pond before continuing their flight to Croespenmaen, where the ghost left Henry to find his way home.

Superstition might well cling to the Glyn Ponds because a few years earlier, in 1868, fourteen people were boating on the lake when the boats sank, hurling the fourteen into the water. Heroic efforts by the rest of the party on the banks meant five were rescued but nine people drowned that day, several of them children.

TINKINSWOOD

GLAMORGANSHIRE

Tinkinswood is a cromlech or burial chamber near the hamlet of St Nicholas, Glamorganshire, on the estate of the family whose house has the honour of being haunted by the ghost of an admiral. Folklore advises that you don't fall asleep at Tinkinswood on any of the three 'spirit nights' of May Day eve, St John's eve (23rd June) or Midwinter eve. If you do, you will either die, go mad, or become a poet. Not very good odds for a positive outcome.

The site is haunted by the spirits of druids who seem to be particularly unkind to drunkards, not to mention other wicked people. One victim said that 'they beat him first, then whirled him up into the sky, from which he looked down and saw the moon and stars thousands of miles below him. They held him suspended by his hair in the midheaven until the first peep of day, and then let him drop down to the Dyffryn woods, where he was found in a great oak by farm labourers.'

Local children call Tinkinswood, Castle Correg, a name which recalls tales of Breton fairies. The korreds and korregs of Brittany closely resemble the Welsh fairies in many details. The korreds are supposed to live in the cromlechs, of which they are believed to have been the builders. They dance around them at night, and woe betide the unhappy peasant who joins them in their roundels.

A group of boulders close by are said to be women who were turned to stone for dancing on the Sabbath. Another legend associated with these boulders states that some women had sworn falsely against an innocent man, who was put to death on gallows on a nearby mountain. On their way home from the hanging, the women were turned to stone.

THE BATTLE OF MYNYDD ABERDARE

There is a tradition among the Glamorgan peasantry of a fairy battle fought on the mountain between Merthyr and Aberdare, in which the pygmy combatants were on horseback. There appeared to be two armies, one of which was mounted on milk-white steeds, and the other on horses of jet-black. They rode at each other with the utmost fury, and their swords could be seen flashing in the air like so many penknife blades. The army on the white horses won the day and drove the black-mounted force from the field. The whole scene then disappeared in a light mist.

ST LYTHANS

CARDIFF

Known locally as Gwal-y-Filiast – Kennel of the Greyhound Bitch - this single stone chamber is all that remains of a once much larger burial monument. The name may come from a variant of the Arthurian legend of Culhwch and Olwen, which appears in two 14th century Welsh texts, but the site itself is very much older, dating from the Neolithic period, some 5,000 to 6,000 years ago.

St Lythans is a type of monument known as a chambered long cairn and was originally covered by an earthen mound, probably similar to that found at its close neighbour, Tinkinswood.

It is said that on Midsummer Eve the stones whirl around three times and go down to the nearby river to bathe.

CARREG LEIDR

ANGLESEY

Just over a century ago, there lived in the parish of Llandyfrydog, near Llannerch y Medd in Anglesey, a man named Ifan Gruffydd, whose cow disappeared one day. Ifan was greatly distressed, and he and his daughter walked up and down the whole neighbourhood in search of her.

As they were coming back in the evening from their unsuccessful quest, they crossed a field called Cae Lleidr Dyfrydog. Suddenly Ifan and his daughter saw a great number of little men on ponies quickly galloping in a ring. They both drew nigh to look on, but Ifan Gruffydd's daughter, in her eagerness to behold the little knights more closely, entered unawares into the circle in which their ponies galloped, and did not return to her father.

Ifan now forgot all about the loss of the cow, and spent some hours searching for his daughter but, at last, he had to go home without her, in the deepest sadness. A few days afterwards, he went to Maenaddwyn to consult John Roberts, who was a magician of no mean reputation. That wise man told Ifan to be sad no longer, since he could get his daughter back at the very hour of the night of the anniversary of the time when he lost her.

He would, in fact, then see her riding round in the company of the Tylwyth Teg, whom he had seen on that memorable night. Ifan was to go there accompanied by four stalwart men, who were to aid him in the rescue of his daughter. He had to tie a strong rope round his waist, and by means of this, his friends could pull him out of the circle once he entered to seize his daughter.

He went to the spot and, in due time, he beheld his daughter riding round in great state. In he rushed and snatched her, and, thanks to his friends, he got her out of the fairy ring before the little men had time to think. The first thing Ifan's daughter asked him was, if he had found the cow, for she had not the slightest reckoning of the time she had spent with the fairies.

This field is called after the Dyfrydog thief. A standing stone remains in the field which legend has it was once a man who stole a Bible from the nearby church. Leaving the church with the Bible, he spotted someone approaching him, so he scuttled into a nearby field to avoid being seen. All to no avail, of course, as the local saint, St Tyfrydog, turned him into stone. Every Christmas Eve, when the stone hears the clock strike twelve, it moves round the field three times.

CARREG HIR

CARMARTHENSHIRE

A more sinister version of this tale comes from Carmarthenshire where Taffy ap Siôn, the shoemaker's son, lived near Pencader. When he was only a lad, he entered the Fairy Circle on the mountain close to his home, and having danced a few minutes, as he supposed, he stepped out of the circle.

To his astonishment, he found that the scene which had been so familiar to him was now quite strange. Here were roads and houses he had never seen, and in place of his father's humble cottage, there now stood a fine stone farmhouse. About him were lovely, cultivated fields instead of the barren mountain he was accustomed to.

'Ah,' thought he, 'this is some Fairy trick to deceive my eyes. It is not ten minutes since I stepped into that circle, and now when I step out, they have built my father a new house! Well, I only hope it is real. Anyhow, I'll go and see.'

So he started off by a path he knew instinctively. Suddenly he struck against a very solid hedge. He rubbed his eyes, felt the hedge with his fingers, scratched his head, felt the hedge again, ran a thorn into his fingers and cried out, 'Wbwb. This is no Fairy hedge anyhow, nor, from the age of the thorns, was it grown in a few minutes' time!'

So he climbed over it and walked on.

'Here was I born,' he said, as he entered the farmyard, staring wildly about him, 'and not a thing here do I know!' His mystification was complete, when there came bounding towards him a huge dog, barking furiously.

'What dog is this? Get out, you ugly brute! Don't you know I'm master here? At least, when Mother's from home, for father don't count.' But the dog only barked the harder. 'Surely,' muttered Taffy to himself, 'I have lost my road and

114

am wandering through some unknown neighbourhood; but no, yonder is the Carreg Hir!" He stood staring at the well-known erect stone thus called, which still stands on the mountain south of Pencader, and is supposed to have been placed there in ancient times to commemorate a victory. As Taffy stood thus, looking at the long stone, he heard footsteps behind him, and turning, saw the occupant of the farmhouse, who had come out to see why his dog was barking. Poor Taffy was so ragged and wan that the farmer's Welsh heart was at once stirred to sympathy.

'Who are you, poor man?' he asked, to which Taffy answered, 'I know who I was, but I do not know who I am now. I was the son of a shoemaker who lived in this place, this morning, for that rock, though it is changed a little, I know too well.'

'Poor fellow,' said the farmer, 'You have lost your senses. This house was built by my great-grandfather, repaired by my grandfather, and that part there, which seems newly built, was done about three years ago at my expense. You must be deranged, or you have missed the road, but come in and refresh yourself with some victuals, and rest.'

Taffy was half persuaded that he had somehow overslept and lost his road, but looking back he saw the rock Carreg Hir, and exclaimed, 'It is but an hour since I was on yonder rock, robbing a hawk's nest.'

'Where have you been since?' asked the farmer. Taffy related his adventure. 'Ah,' said the farmer, 'I see how it is. You have been with the Fairies. Pray who was your father?'

'Siôn Evan y Crydd o Glanrhyd,' Taffy answered.

'I never heard of such a man,' said the farmer, shaking his head, 'nor of such a place as Glanrhyd, either. But no matter. After you have taken a little food, we will step down to Catti Shon, at Pencader, who will probably be able to tell something.'

With this, he beckoned Taffy to follow him and walked on. Hearing behind him the sound of footsteps growing weaker and weaker, he turned round and, to his horror, beheld the poor fellow crumble in an instant to about a thimbleful of black ashes. The farmer, though very terrified at this sight, kept sufficiently calm to go at once and see old Catti, the aged crone he had referred to, who lived at Pencader, near by. He found her crouching over a fire of faggots, trying to warm her old bones.

'And how do you do the day, Catti Shon?' asked the farmer. 'Ah,' said old Catti, 'I'm wonderful well, farmer, considering how old I am.'

'Yes, yes, you are very old. Now, since you are so old, let me ask you. Do you remember anything about Siôn y Crydd o Glanrhyd? Was there ever such a man, do you know?'

'Siôn Glanrhyd? Oh! I have a faint recollection of hearing my grandfather, old Evan Shenkin Penferdir, relate that Siôn's son was lost one morning, and they never heard of him afterwards, so that it was said he was taken by the Fairies. His father's cottage stood somewhere near your house.'

'Were there many Fairies about at that time?' asked the farmer.

'Oh, yes, they were often seen on yonder hill, and I was told they were lately seen in Pant Shon Shenkin, eating flummery out of egg-shells, which they had stolen from a farm hard by.'

'Dir anwyl fi!' cried the farmer, 'dear me! I recollect now I saw them myself.'

MOEL EILIO

CAERNARFONSHIRE

A Bronze Age cairn on the top of Moel Eilio is said to belong to the fairies, the Tylwyth Teg of Nant y Bettws, who live in hidden caves within the mountain. If anyone comes across the mouth of their cave, they will find there a wonderful amount of wealth, 'for they were thieves without their like'.

One fine sunny morning, as the young heir of Ystrad was busy with his sheep on the side of Moel Eilio, he met a very pretty girl, and when he returned home, he told the folks there of it. A few days afterwards, he met her again. This happened several times, and when he mentioned it to his father, he advised him to seize her when he next met her.

The next time he met her, he proceeded to do so, but before he could take her away, a little fat old man came to them and begged him to give her back to him, to which the youth would not listen. The little man uttered terrible threats but he would not yield, so an agreement was made between them that he was to have her to wife until he touched her skin with iron, and great was the joy, both of the son and his parents.

They lived together for many years, but once, on the evening of Bettws Fair, the wife's horse got restive, and somehow, as the husband was attending to the horse, the stirrups touched the skin of her bare leg. That very night, she was taken away from him. She had three or four children, and more than one of their descendants, as the story writer and poet Glasynys, the Bardic name of Owen Wynne Jones, maintains, were known to him at the time he wrote in 1863.

CARREG Y BWCI

LAMPETER

The Goblin Stone is located on a lonely moorland ridge by Lampeter, next to the Sarn Helen Roman road. Theories about the site and its original function suggest it was possibly a round barrow, a chambered tomb or even a Roman watchtower.

Few would pass the stone at night. In the 17th century, a young man in search of work made the mistake of sleeping next to it. At midnight, someone pinching his arms and ears and pricking his nose woke him. By the dim light of the stars, he saw the form of a goblin sitting on the stone with a few others around him.

The young man tried to make his escape, but the chief goblin ordered his minions to hold him back. They tormented him until first light, at which point the goblins simply vanished. When the unfortunate man related his story to some passers-by, he was informed he had slept under the haunted goblin stone.

The stone is also said to attract lightning strikes and three men were killed here during a thunderstorm. Lightning strikes are attached to treasure and hoard lore. To touch or dig for buried treasure guarded by a ghost, without the ghost's consent, will always bring thunder and lightning. Such is the tradition in connection with Carreg y Bwci.

The stone to this day is still associated with mysterious occurrences. Horses fear passing the place, with recent reports of bolting horses and unusual mists.

LLYS HELIG

LLANDUDNO

On the north western tip of mainland Wales is a mysterious rock formation. This massive headland to the west of Llandudno Bay is called by the English the Great Orme. The word *Orme* is thought to derive from the Scandinavian word for a worm. It is said that a Viking raiding party saw the rock rearing up from the mist in front of their longboat and mistaking it for a serpent, fled in terror.

At the end of the last Ice Age, retreating glaciers left behind many strangely shaped rocks around the Orme; the Mother and Daughter Stones, The Freetrade Loaf, The Rocking Stone and many others. Each stone appears to have its own story attached to it!

Amongst the many legends associated with the Great Orme is the story of Llys Helig (Helig's Palace) and the lost Land of Tyno Helig.

Tyno Helig is said to have been a Welsh kingdom, situated on the low coastal plain to the west of the Great Orme and run by Prince Helig ap Glannawg in the 6th century from Llys Helig (Helig's Palace). One legend tells of Helig's daughter, Gwendud, who was beautiful and cruel. She refused to marry her betrothed, Tahal, a Snowdonian nobleman's son, unless he acquired a high-status golden collar.

After offering to guide a ransomed young Scottish chieftain back to safety, Tahal treacherously stabbed him and stole his golden collar. He claimed they had been set upon by a band of robbers headed by an outlaw nobleman, whom he had slain in fair fight.

Gwendud now consented to marry Tahal, and Prince Helig ordering a great feast to celebrate the union. At some point in the proceedings, the ghost of the murdered Scottish chieftain appeared and informed them that he would exact a terrible vengeance over four generations of their family.

Despite the curse, it is said that Gwendud and Tahal lived well into their old age. Retribution appears to have caught up with the family with the birth of their great-great-grandchild. During a night of celebration and revelry in the royal palace, a maid went down into the cellar to bring up more wine. She was horrified to discover that the cellar was flooded with fish swimming around in the salty seawater. Quickly realising something serious had occurred, she and her lover, who was the court minstrel, ran for the safety of the mountains. They were hardly out of the banqueting hall when they heard shrieks of terror from behind them. Looking back, they could see the foam of mighty breaking waves racing towards them. With water lapping at their heels, they ran until at last they reached the safety of the land. Breathless and exhausted, they waited for the morning. When the sun rose, it disclosed an expanse of rippling water where Helig's Palace had once stood.

It is said that, at very low tides, the ruins of the old palace can still be seen under the water. There is an area on the western slopes of the Orme, overlooking Conwy Bay, which to this day is known as Llys Helig.

A similar tale of a drowned kingdom tells of Cantre'r Gwaelod in Cardiganshire, which had sixteen wealthy towns, the most prestigious of which was Manua. The towns were all protected by dykes or sea walls. The land was drained at low tide by opening sluice gates, which were closed as the tide began to rise, a task overseen by a watchman.

One night, the spring tide was whipped into a frenzy by a bad storm and beat against the sea walls. Instead of tending the open sluice gate, the appointed watchman, the

King's knight Seithenyn, was attending revels in the King's palace. His absence doomed the land. As the sea rushed in, the King escaped with some of the revellers along the Sarn Cynfelyn causeway, which remains today, and the farmers and villagers were driven away from their rich lands into the far poorer fields and hills behind Cardigan Bay.

Another version agrees that Seithenyn was at the King's palace at the time of the storm, but that he had left a girl named Mererid in charge of the sluice gates. Seithenyn seduced Mererid who failed to close the sluice gates, causing the lands to be submerged beneath the sea.

A different legend says that a fairy well was located near the land, tended to by a priestess. For reasons unknown, she decided to allow the well to overflow, with the same consequences.

Finally, another tradition has it that a giant called Idris Gawr, whose throne was Cadair Idris, roamed the hills around Aberdyfi, carrying a massive bell. He liked to paddle and so sometimes left his mountain eyrie to stride in the waters of the River Dyfi. One day he was surprised by a great storm and drowned, but his bell continues to ring to this day.

All versions of the legend agree that if you listen carefully, particularly on a quiet night, a Sunday morning or in times of danger, the bells of Cantre'r Gwaelod can still be heard from Aberdyfi and Ynys-las, ringing under the sea.

THE DRAGON OF THE FALLS

LLANRHAEADR

The Dragon of Llanrhaeadr at Pistyll Rhaeadr is a great Welsh legend where good triumphs over evil.

The winged snake, called a Gwybr, lived in the lake called Llyn Luncaws above the waterfall. Once every few days, the Gwybr would fly down the valley to the village and there seize children, women or animals, taking them back to the lake to devour them.

The people of the village got together and, as nobody knew how to kill the Gwybr, several villagers walked over the mountains for many days to reach the wise woman of the hills. They told her the frightening story and she listened in silence. When they were finished, she bade them sleep whilst she thought on the problem.

Next morning, when the villagers awoke, she explained to them what they had to do when they got home. As soon as they arrived back, the men got together and went to the blacksmith's shop, where they worked all day and all night creating three enormous, spiked collars of different sizes. The women worked together and gathered in all the linen in the village, sewed it together to make a huge sheet and dyed it blood-red.

When all was ready, the whole village set off to the tumuli and great standing stone in the field at the foot of Rhos Brithin. Here the men dropped the three spiked collars over the pillar and the women wrapped the whole lot in the red linen. Then they set about building a circle of fire round the pillar.

Soon the Gwybr was sighted on its way down the river. Quickly they lit the fire and hid amongst the bushes and hedges to watch. As it approached the village, the great serpent was attracted by the fire and, as it flew closer, it thought it saw another dragon illuminated by the flickering flames. It roared with anger and threw itself to the attack, spearing its breast on the hidden spikes.

Again and again, it attacked and each time the spikes drove deeper into its body until it dripped with blood and grew weaker. Eventually it could fight no more and collapsed, bleeding and dying, at the foot of the pillar.

Once more the village was safe.

At 80m, Pistyll Rhaeadr is the UK's highest single drop waterfall and is considerably higher than Niagara Falls. It's always enchanting and, on rare occasions, it freezes into an ice sculpture.

THE SHADOW

LLANBERIS (JACK'S TALE)

I was babysitting my niece once while I was staying at my brother's place, in Llanberis and they had the baby camera set up so I could see her on the little monitor. I was studying and started dozing off when I heard some whispering and realised it was coming from the monitor.

I initially thought it was feedback or something, but when I looked at the monitor, there was a dark shadow near my niece's crib.

I have never been more terrified in my life, but the shadow was clearly there where it had not been before. I ran to my niece's room and looked around but, seeing nothing, I took her the hell out of there. I went back to the monitor, and the shadow was clearly gone.

I told my brother what had happened and he pulled me aside and told me not to mention it to my sister-in-law because she'd freak out, but that he had seen that same thing several times now, with the same whispering.

They stayed in that house for about four more years and when my niece was just learning to talk, she would tell her mam about her 'special friend'. To this day, it scares the c**p out of me.

When they moved out, my brother told me my niece had become inconsolably sad because she would miss her 'friend'. Her mam would tell her she could bring him along but all she would say was that he couldn't leave the house. We have never to this day told her about that damn shadow, and she apparently never saw it again.

FFYNNON FAIR

THE RHONDDA

Ffynnon Fair, St Mary's Well, is a holy well on the hillside overlooking the village of Llwynypia. The well has long been the focus of religious activity in Penrhys and is the oldest recorded Christian site in the Rhondda. Some historians believe the site may date back further and could be pagan in origin. The waters from the well were believed to have the ability to cure ailments, particularly rheumatism and poor eyesight, and were reported by the poet Rhisiart ap Rhys as:

> There are rippling waters at the top of the rock
> Farewell to every ailment that desires them!
> White wine runs in the rill,
> That can kill pain and fatigue!

There is a legend that a statue of the Virgin Mary appeared in the branches of an oak tree close to the well. It was said to have been incredibly beautiful and a gift from Heaven. The statue resisted all attempts to remove it from the tree, until a chapel and shrine were built. It is said that the statue survived at Penrhys until 1538, when King Henry VIII's dissolution of the monasteries brought the destruction of the shrine, and the public burning of the statue in London along with other religious artefacts.

The vaulted stone building, built around the well, still exists today, although heavily restored. It is entirely built of local pennant sandstone, with one side built into the sloping hillside. The interior of the small rectangular building consists of stone benches around three walls, a cistern occupying the south wall. A niche in the north wall was said to have held the statue of Mary. The floor is paved with dressed flagstones.

A WATERY GRAVE

MID WALES

I didn't grow up believing in ghosts. Then one morning when we were 16, when my friend's mam picked us up, I mentioned I was really creeped out by this bathroom under the stairs in my house that no one ever used. I couldn't exactly define why I felt this way; I just found it eerie.

The house I grew up in was an old Victorian home, built in the 1800s, so eerie vibes were part of the package. Hearing this reminded my friend of her own creepy bathroom association.

She told me that when she lived in the Mid Wales countryside for a year, there was a little section in the home only used by her middle sister, who was about nine years old at the time. During this time, her sister would wake up with bloodshot eyes, sometimes even bruises, and feel totally exhausted.

They did everything to investigate what was going on, including sleeping in her room, working with a child psychologist, and a school counsellor. My friend doesn't remember much from this time, other than her sister being disturbed by something during the year they lived there.

She mentioned that she and her other sister, the oldest, also hated using that bathroom because they would always feel 'off' and find thick black hairs stuck in the drain, even though each of them had fine blond hair. At this point in the story, my friend's mam abruptly stopped the car and jerked her head around and said, 'That's where the woman [who once lived there] killed herself. She drowned herself in that bathtub.' Her mam was clearly shaken. She said part of the reason they moved was because something felt 'off' in the house.

MAN'S BEST FRIEND

CARDIFF UNIVERSITY

While studying at Cardiff University, a student had a dog that was super-loyal and loving and would always come running when he was called, almost crashing into his owner whenever he had treats for him.

One day, as they were both sitting in the living room, all the hair on the dog's back stood up and he was just staring, growling and showing his teeth.

No matter what the student did to try to get him to stop, he never stopped staring at that one spot and just kept growling. Eventually the student carried him out of the room because it was freaking everyone there out so badly.

KIM'S BASEMENT

NEWPORT

This story was related by Kim:

I lived once in a Newport house with a basement and every time I walked up the stairs, I would get this weird, creepy goosebumps feeling on the back of my neck. It didn't make me uneasy to go down the stairs or to be in the basement.

My craft room was down there I and I spent a lot of time there. After a while, I would have items I was using disappear when I would look away from them. I would search and search and one day I got frustrated and to no one in particular, I said, 'Arrrgh!! Can I please have my scissors back?'

I had just looked under the pile of new mail and when I turned my head, there were my scissors on top of the pile of mail. I talked to my neighbour and she told me that the original owner of the house was a jolly old man who loved to prank people and that he had fallen coming up the stairs one day and died. I think the goosebumps were him trying to tell me to be careful! And every time after that, when something would disappear, I would politely ask for it back and it would appear in a place that I could not have missed it before! Thanks, old man, it was fun!

ABOUT THE AUTHOR

Nic was born and raised in Cwmbran, South Wales, and was married in Wrexham, North Wales. Nic writes Welsh Poetry and Welsh Legends and Ghost stories. This is now his tenth book. He has been married to Karen for 21 years, and is blessed with a son, Ben Llewelyn. Nic loves all things about Wales.

ABOUT THE PUBLISHERS

Saron Publishers has been in existence since 2000, producing niche magazines. Our first venture into books took place in 2016 when we published *The Meanderings of Bing* by Tim Harnden-Taylor. Further publications include *Minstrel Magic,* by Eleanor Pritchard, choirmaster George Mitchell's biography, *Penthusiasm,* a collection of short stories and poems from Penthusiasts, a writing group based in the beautiful town of Usk, and *Frank,* a gentle novel about loss, by Julie Hamill, followed in 2019 but its sequel *Jackie.*

2019 also saw the publication, among others, of Kevin Moore's second book, *Real Murder Investigations – An Insider's View,* which delves in more detail into some cases mentioned in his previous book, *My Way.*

Recent publications have included Kevin's third book *Good Cop, Bad Cop,* as well as *The Best of Times* by Eugene Barter, one-time secretary to Sir Edward Heath, *Patron Saints of Gwent* and *A War Time Log,* the POW diaries of John Davies Jones.

Join our mailing list at info@ saronpublishers.co.uk. We promise no spam ever.

Visit our website saronpublishers.co.uk to keep up to date and to read reviews of what we've been reading and enjoying. You can also enjoy the occasional offer of a free Bing chapter.

Follow us on Facebook @saronpublishing.
Follow us on Twitter @saronpublishers.

INDEX OF PLACE NAMES

Manufactured by Amazon.ca
Bolton, ON

42000188R00079